a dream?

He awoke with a start, his body drenched with sweat. Gabriel had joined him on the bed, and his dark brown eyes glistened eerily in a strange light that danced around the room.

"Gabriel, what . . . ?" he began breathlessly.

"Nice sword," the dog said simply.

Fully awake now, Aaron realized that he held something in his left hand. Slowly he turned his gaze toward it—toward what he had brought back from the realm of nightmare.

A blade of the sun.

the fallen

Book Two

leviathan

Thomas E. Sniegoski

Simon Pulse
NEW YORK   LONDON   TORONTO   SYDNEY   SINGAPORE

First Simon Pulse edition July 2003

Copyright © 2003 by Thomas E. Sniegoski

SIMON PULSE
An imprint of Simon & Schuster
Children's Publishing Division
1230 Avenue of the Americas
New York, NY 10020

Designed by Sammy Yuen Jr.
The text of this book was set in 11 point Palatino.

Printed in the United States of America
4 6 8 10 9 7 5 3

Library of Congress Control Number 2002112879

ISBN 0-689-85306-8

For Tobi and all the other special friends lost to us. You will always be missed and never be far from our hearts; best friends forever.

As always, this book could not have been possible without the loving support of my wife, LeeAnne, and the daily inspiration provided to me by Mulder, the King of the Labs (or so he believes).

A special tip of the hat to my partner in crime, Christopher Golden, and to Lisa Clancy and her assistant to die for, Lisa Gribbin.

And special thanks are also due to Mom and Dad, Eric "the Goon" Powell, Dave Kraus, David Carroll, Dr. Kris, Tom and Lorie Stanley, Paul Griffin, Tim Cole and the usual cast of characters, Jon and Flo, Bob and Pat, Don Kramer, Pete Donaldson, Kristy Bratton, and Ken Curtis for the use of his name. Thank you one and all, good night, and drive carefully.

prologue

$\mathcal{A}$midst the south Serbian Mountains, nestled within the gorge of the Black River, sat the Crna Reka Monastery. The wind howled piteously, like the sad wails of a mother mourning the loss of her child, as it blew across the high rocks and sparse vegetation surrounding the holy hermitage.

It was a lonely place, a place for reflection and absolution. The church itself was constructed within a large cave during the thirteenth century— a homage to the Archangel Michael. The hermit monks soon built their cells around the church, and a small drawbridge was erected over the Black River. By a great blessing of God, the river disappeared underground just before the monastery, and then reappeared several hundred meters later, sparing the monastery the deafening roar of the water's noise.

The repenter knelt upon a worn, wicker mat in

a cold, empty room of the monastery in the rocks, and listened to the prayers of the world. No matter the time, be it day or night, someone, somewhere, searched for the aid or guidance of the Divine. A woman in Prague prayed for the soul of her recently departed mother, a man in Glasgow for the continued health of his wife stricken with cancer. A farmer in Fort Wayne asked for relief from a fearsome drought, and a truck driver parked alongside a road in Scottsdale begged for the strength to live his life another day. So many voices, a cacophony of cries for help—it made his head spin.

He tried to lend them all a slight bit of his own strength, and asked the Creator to listen to their pleas. *Does the Lord of Lords hear me?* he wondered. The penitent hoped so. Though others would have him believe that the Holy Father had stopped listening to him a long time ago, it did not prevent him from speaking on behalf of those who prayed—a conduit to Heaven.

Eyes tightly closed, ears filled with the sounds of benediction, the kneeling man smiled. A six-year-old named Kiley prayed with the passion of a saint for a brand-new bike on her birthday. Had he ever prayed with such fervor for anything? The answer was obvious—it was the reason he continued to wander the planet, searching out the most sacred places, hoping to quell the burning turmoil at the core of his being.

The sinner sought forgiveness—forgiveness for the evil he had wrought.

The sound of tiny claws scrabbling across the stone floor wrested him from his concentration, and he opened his eyes. A mouse stood on its hindquarters, nose twitching eagerly toward him.

"Well, hello there," the penitent said softly, his voice filled with affection for the gray-furred rodent. He and the mouse had become good friends since his arrival at the monastery six months before. And in exchange for bits of bread and cheese, the little animal kept him abreast of events outside the hermitage.

From within the long sleeves of his robe, the repenter produced a crust of bread from the previous night's supper and offered it to the small creature. *"And how are you today?"* he asked in a language only it would understand.

"Others here," the mouse replied in a high-pitched squeak as it took the bread in its front paws.

For the last two months he had sensed something growing in the ether, building steadily over the past few days. Something with the potential for great danger—and yet also wondrous. He had his suspicions, but did not want to get his hopes up only to have them dashed to pieces again.

"Others like you," the mouse finished, nervously gnawing on the piece of bread.

Suddenly the repenter was glad that he had sent the Crna Reka brothers to town for supplies this day. If what the mouse was telling him was true, he did not wish to risk the well-being of anyone else. The brothers had been quite gracious in allowing him into their place of quiet solitude, and he did not want to see any of them suffer for their charity.

He listened, focusing on the sounds of the monastery around him: the muffled roar of the Black River flowing beneath the structure; the creak of the bridge outside, jostled by the winds blowing into the gorge from the mountains above; the rumble of thunder.

No, not thunder at all, something far more ominous.

The penitent picked the mouse up from the floor and placed it in his palm as he stood. *"And where exactly did you see these others?"* he asked.

"Outside," it answered, continuing its nibbling. *"In sky. Outside in sky."*

It was then that the repenter began to feel their presence. They were all around him. The floor of the monastery began to shake, as if in the clutches of an angry giant. Rock, dust, and wood fell from the ceiling, and the walls began to crumble. He clutched the tiny life-form to his breast to protect it from the falling debris. An explosion, filled with sound and fury, rocked the monastery, and the walls before him fell away, sliding into the Black River Gorge to reveal the

Serbian Mountains, and those who awaited him.

They hovered there, at least twenty in number, their mighty wings beating the air—the sound like the racing heartbeat of the wilderness valley surrounding them—and in their hands they held weapons of fire.

The repenter stepped back from the jagged edge of a yawning precipice and held the trembling mouse closer. He did not take his eyes from them. He was not afraid. Some bowed their heads as his gaze fell upon them, remembering a bygone time when he had commanded their respect—but that was long, long ago.

"Lift your heads," ordered an angry voice in the language of messengers. Their numbers began to part, and he who led them moved forward. *"The time for this one to be shown reverence passed when the first seeds of the Great War were sown."*

The penitent was familiar with he who spoke: a wrathful angel in the Choir called Powers. His name was Verchiel, and he bore the scars of one who had recently fought a fierce battle. The repenter wondered why they had not healed, and almost asked the angel—but decided this was not the time.

"We have come for you, son of the morning," Verchiel said, pointing his sword that burned like the heart of an inferno.

With those words, the angels of the Powers glided closer, their weapons raised for conflict.

"Your corrupting time upon God's world has ended," Verchiel said with a gleam in his deep, dark eyes of solid night.

"You'll receive no fight from me," the repenter replied, looking from the fearsome Powers drawing inexorably closer to the mouse still held in his hand against his chest. *"Just keep your voices down,"* he continued as he ran a finger along the soft, downy fur of the trembling rodent's head. *"You're scaring the mouse."*

"Take him!" Verchiel cried in a voice that hinted of madness, scars hot and red against his pale flesh.

And they flew at him.

The repenter did as he imagined he must. No weapons of fire sprang from his palms, no powerful wings unfurled to carry him away. He slipped the fragile creature that had become his friend inside the folds of his simple robes, and let himself be taken.

Shackles of a golden metal not found on this world, their surface etched in an angelic spell of suppression, were slapped roughly upon his wrists, and he felt himself immediately sapped of strength by their inherent magick. Some of the Powers, but not all, clawed at him, striking him, beating him with their wings—even though he offered no resistance. The penitent could understand their resentment and did nothing to halt their abuse.

"Enough!" Verchiel bellowed, and the angelic soldiers stepped away from the repenter's prone form on what remained of the room's floor.

The leader of the Powers approached, and the prisoner looked up into his cold, merciless gaze. *"So angry,"* he whispered as he studied the expression of cruelty burned upon the angelic commander's face. *"So filled with blind hatred. I've seen that look before. It's very familiar to me."*

Verchiel motioned for his men to lift the repenter from the ground, and they did just that—but he continued to examine the leader's troubling features.

"I used to see it every time I saw my reflection," he said as he was borne aloft by the angels of the Powers.

His words struck a sensitive chord. Verchiel's expression changed to one of unbridled fury, and he lunged toward the repenter, a new weapon of flame taking shape. *Will it be a sword to cleave my skull in two—or maybe a battle-ax to separate my head from my shoulders?* he wondered. The weapon became a mace, and the angel swung with a force that would shatter mountains. It connected with the side of the prisoner's head, and an explosion, very much like the birth of a galaxy, blossomed behind his eyes.

As he slipped into the void, he was accompanied by the fading sounds of the world he was leaving behind, the murmurs of prayer, the moan of the mountain winds, the pounding wings of vengeful angels, and the rapid-fire beating of a frightened mouse's heart.

Then, for a time, all was blissfully silent.

chapter one

Aaron Corbet accelerated to seventy mph on I-95 heading north. He turned up the volume on the cassette player and casually glanced to the right to see the angel Camael wincing as if in pain.

"What's wrong?" Aaron asked. "Do you sense something? What is it?"

The angel shook his head, his expression wrinkling with distaste. "The noise," he said, pointing a slender finger at the dashboard cassette player. "It brings tears to my eyes."

Aaron smiled. "Oh, you like it?"

"No," the angel grumbled as he shook his head. "It pains me."

"It's the Dave Matthews Band!" Aaron exclaimed, genuinely stunned.

"I don't care whose band it is," the angel growled, moving agitatedly about in the passenger seat. "It makes my eyes water."

Annoyed, Aaron hit the eject button, and the cassette slowly emerged with a soft, mechanical whir. "There," he said, gripping the steering wheel with both hands. "Is that better?"

The radio had come on, and the sound of Top 40 pop filled the vehicle. One of the popular boy bands—he could never tell them apart—was singing about lost love. He glanced again at Camael to see that the angel was still making a face.

"What's wrong now? I turned off my music."

"And I am appreciative," the angel warrior said as he gazed out the window at the scenery whipping past. "But I find all of your so-called music to be extremely discordant. It offends my senses."

Gabriel reared up in the back and stuck his yellow-white snout between the front seats. *"I like the song about Tasty Chow,"* the dog said.

Happy to be talking about anything that can end up in his stomach, Aaron thought as he squeezed the steering wheel in both hands.

"How does that song go, Aaron?" the Labrador retriever asked. *"I've forgotten."*

"I don't know, Gabriel," he said, becoming more irritated. "That's not even a real song—it's a dog food jingle, a commercial."

"I don't care," the dog said indignantly. *"I like that song a lot—and the commercial is good too. It's got kids and puppies, and they play on swings and run and jump and then the puppies eat Tasty Chow. . . ."*

Gabriel stopped mid-sentence as Aaron reached out to shut off the radio, plunging the car into silence. *Great*, he thought as he drove, *just what I need*. Without the distraction of music, his wandering mind had another opportunity to examine how completely insane his life had become.

Just over two weeks ago, on his eighteenth birthday, Aaron learned he was something called a Nephilim—the child of a human mother and an angel. Aaron never knew his biological parents, having been in foster care all his life. So when he began to exhibit rather unique abilities, like being able to speak and understand foreign languages—human and animal—he thought that maybe he was losing his mind.

Which was exactly what he was going to do if he didn't stop thinking about this stuff. He glanced over at the powerfully built man—*no, angel*—sitting in the passenger seat beside him. "So what kind of music do you like?" he asked to break the silence.

Camael had once been the leader of an army—a Choir of angels, the Powers, whose purpose it was to eliminate all things offensive to God. After Lucifer's defeat in the Great War in Heaven, many of his followers fled to Earth. Barred from Heaven, these angels began a life upon the world of man, some even taking wives and having children. It was the job of the Powers to destroy these defectors and their abominable offspring, the Nephilim.

"You are speaking to one who has heard the symphony of Creation," the angel said in a condescending tone. "How can the sounds produced by the likes of your primitive species even compare?"

As Aaron knew, on one of his many missions to eradicate the enemies of Heaven, Camael had been made privy to a prophecy—a prophecy that described a creature, both human and angel, that would reestablish a bond between the fallen angels on Earth and God. This being—a Nephilim—would forgive these angels their sins and allow their return to Heaven. After so much violence and death, Camael thought this was truly a great thing, but his opinion was not shared by his second-in-command, a nasty piece of work that went by the name of Verchiel.

"So you don't like any of it?" Aaron asked, dumbfounded by the angel's broad dismissal of the entire musical spectrum. "You don't like classical or jazz—or rock or country? None of it? Everything gives you a headache?"

The angel looked at him, eyes burning with intensity. "I haven't had the time to sample all forms of your music," he said. "As you are aware, I have been rather busy."

Camael left the Powers to follow the prophecy. For thousands of years he wandered the planet, attempting to save the lives of Nephilim—hoping that each might be the one of which the prophecy foretold. Now led by

Verchiel, the Powers would do anything to eliminate the blight of half-breeds from God's world, making the prophecy but an ancient memory.

"But you've been here forever," Aaron said with a disbelieving grin. "I don't mean to be a pain in the ass, but . . ."

"That's exactly what you are, boy," Camael said, looking back out the side window. "You are the One—as well as a pain in the ass."

So besides being a Nephilim, which was bad enough, Aaron Corbet was also the subject of the prophecy. It wasn't something he had even been aware of—until the Powers, under Verchiel's command, attempted to kill him. The attacks resulted in the deaths of his psychiatrist, his foster parents and a fallen angel by the name of Zeke—who had helped him finally tap into his angelic abilities and save himself.

"I'm sorry," Aaron said, slowing down as a red sports car pulled up alongside him on the two-lane road, then sped up to pass. "It's just that you come off all holier-than-thou because you're an angel and everything—when in fact you really don't know what you're talking about."

"Though I no longer associate with their Choir, I am of the Powers," Camael said, "one of the first created by God, and it is my right to have an opinion that disagrees with yours."

The abilities called to life with Zeke's urgings saved not only Aaron's life, but also the life of his dog, Gabriel. When the Labrador was struck by a car and mortally injured, Aaron called upon his latent powers and healed the dog, as a result changing Gabriel into something more than just a dog.

"You can't have a real opinion unless you've actually listened to the stuff. It's like saying you don't like broccoli when you've never even tasted it," he said, frustrated by the angel's attitude.

"*I like broccoli,*" Gabriel said suddenly. "*I wish I had some right now. All that talk about Tasty Chow has made me very hungry.*"

Aaron glanced at the digital clock on the dashboard. It was a little before noon. They had been on the road since the crack of dawn, and it had been a long time since breakfast. *Maybe we should pull over and get something to eat,* he thought. Then he remembered Stevie and immediately felt guilty. Who knew what was happening to his foster brother?

When the Powers attacked his home, the angels took his seven-year-old foster brother. Stevie was autistic, and according to Camael, angelic beings often used the handicapped as servants because of their unique sensitivity to the supernatural. This was the main reason they were on the road, to rescue Stevie—that and to prevent the Powers from hurting anyone else Aaron might care about.

Aaron was distracted by the sound of something spattering and looked down near the emergency break to see saliva pooling from Gabriel's mouth. "Gabriel," he scolded, reaching back to push the dog into his seat, "you're drooling!"

"I told you I was hungry," the Lab said, leaning back. *"I can't stop thinking about that Tasty Chow commercial."*

Aaron looked over at Camael, who was silent as he gazed stoically out the window. "So what do you think?" he asked. "I'm getting kind of hungry myself. Should we stop and get some lunch?"

"It makes no difference to me," the angel said, not looking at him. "I have no need of food."

Aaron chuckled. "You know, that's right," he said, the realization sinking home. "I've never seen you eat."

"I love to eat," said Gabriel from the back.

"How is that possible?" Aaron asked, finding himself interested in yet another aspect of the alien life-form known as angel. "Everything has to eat to survive—or is this some bizarre kind of supernatural nonsense that I won't understand?"

"We feed off the energies of life," Camael explained. "Everything that is alive radiates energy—we are like plants to the sun, absorbing this energy to maintain life."

Aaron thought about that for a moment. "So, since you're sitting here with me and Gabe—you could say you're eating right now?"

The angel nodded. "You could say that."

"*I'm not eating right now, although I wish I was,*" the dog said irritably.

"Okay, okay," Aaron replied, preparing to take the next exit. "We'll find someplace for a quick bite, but then we have to get back on the road. I don't want Stevie with those murdering sons of bitches any longer than he has to be."

As he took the exit and merged right, onto a smaller, more secluded stretch of road, Aaron thought about all he had left behind. Every stretch of highway, every exit, every back road took him farther and farther away from the life he was used to. He already found himself missing school, something he hadn't thought possible. It was senior year, after all, and in some perverse way he had been looking forward to all of the final papers and tests, the acceptances and rejections from colleges. But that was not to be; being born a Nephilim had seen to that.

Aaron caught sight of a roadside stand advertising fried clams, hamburgers, and hot dogs. There were picnic tables set up in a shaded area nearby—perfect for Gabriel.

As he pulled into the dirt lot, an image of Vilma came to mind. Before his life collapsed, he had almost believed that he was going to go out with one of the prettiest girls he had ever seen. They never did have an opportunity for that lunch date, and now probably never would. Suddenly Aaron wasn't quite as hungry as he had been.

† † †

Vilma Santiago sat at the far end of the cafeteria at Kenneth Curtis High School and was glad to be alone. It was a beautiful spring day, and most of the student body had taken their lunches outside, so she'd had no difficulty finding an empty table.

The elusive memory of the previous night's dream—*or was it a nightmare?*—teased her with its slippery evasiveness. She hadn't slept well for days, and it was finally beginning to affect her. The girl felt tired, irritable, with the hint of a headache, its pulsing pain just behind her eyes.

But most of all, she felt sad.

Vilma opened the paper sack that contained her lunch and removed a yogurt and a sandwich wrapped in plastic. She had been in such a state that morning, she couldn't even remember what kind of sandwich she'd made. She hoped the lunches she'd prepared for her niece and nephew were at least edible, or she would be hearing from her aunt when she got home.

Without bothering to check the contents of the sandwich, she placed it back inside the bag. *The yogurt'll be plenty*, she thought as she removed the plastic lid and then realized that she didn't have a spoon.

It was no big deal, there were plenty of plastic spoons at the condiment table—but the intense, irrational disappointment of the moment made her want to cry.

Vilma had been feeling a bit emotional since

Aaron Corbet left school—left the state, for all she knew—a couple of weeks ago. She had no idea why she missed him so much. She had just barely gotten to know him.

She placed the lid back on the yogurt and pushed that away as well. She really didn't feel like eating, anyway.

There was something about Aaron, something she couldn't quite understand, but a kind of comfort and calmness seemed to envelop her whenever he was around. Though they had never been on a date—or even held hands, for that matter—Vilma felt as though a very important part of her had been surgically removed with Aaron's departure. She felt incomplete. She wanted to believe that it was a silly crush, a teenage infatuation that would eventually fade, but something inside her said it wasn't, and that just made her all the more miserable.

Vilma sat back in her chair, looked out over the cafeteria, and unconsciously played with the angel that hung on a gold chain around her neck.

According to the news reports, Aaron's foster parents and little brother had died in a fire when their house had been hit by lightning during a freak thunderstorm. He'd said he was leaving because there were too many sad memories. But she'd known he was holding something back—although she didn't know how or why she knew this. Not for the first time she felt her eyes begin to burn with emotion.

There had been talk at school, silly hurtful whispers, that Aaron had been responsible for the fire that took the lives of his family, but Vilma didn't believe it for a second. Sure, he was a foster kid who'd been shifted around a lot. He was entitled to be angry. But, she knew in the depths of her soul that he wasn't capable of harming anyone. Still, the mystery of his abrupt departure continued to gnaw at her.

Vilma jumped as a voice suddenly addressed her. She had been so lost in her thoughts that she'd failed to notice the approach of one of the cafeteria staff.

"I'm sorry, hon," said the large woman with a smile. She was dressed in a light blue uniform, her bleached blond hair tucked beneath a hairnet. "I didn't mean to scare you."

"That's all right," Vilma answered with an embarrassed laugh. "Just not paying attention, I guess."

"You done here?" the woman asked, gesturing to Vilma's discarded lunch.

"Yes, thank you," she replied as the woman swiped a damp cloth across the table and carried away her trash.

Vilma continued to sit, gently stroking the golden angel at her throat. Maybe that was why she hadn't been sleeping. Since Aaron left, her nights had been plagued with dim nightmares. She'd awaken in the early morning hours, panicked and covered in sweat, the recollection of what had caused such a reaction a nagging unknown.

That had to be it. Not only had Aaron made her sad by leaving, he was now keeping her awake with bad dreams. She wished he were here so she could give him a piece of her mind. And when she was done, she'd hold him tightly and they would kiss.

Vilma imagined what that would be like and felt her heart begin to race and her eyes well with tears.

"Vilma!" somebody called, the voice echoing around the low-ceilinged lunchroom.

She rubbed at her eyes quickly and looked around. From a door in the back corner, she saw her friend Tina heading toward her. The girl was wearing dark sunglasses and walked as if she were on the runway at a Paris fashion show. Vilma smiled and waved.

"What are you doing in here?" Tina asked in their native Portuguese.

Vilma shrugged. "I don't know," she answered sadly. "Just didn't feel like going out."

Tina pushed the sunglasses back onto her head and crossed her arms. "I bet you didn't even eat lunch," she said, a look of disgust on her pretty face.

Vilma was about to tell her otherwise but didn't have the strength. "No," she said, her fingers again going to the golden cherub. "I wasn't hungry."

Tina stared at her, saying nothing, and Vilma began to feel self-conscious. She wondered if her eyes showed that she'd been crying.

"What?" Vilma asked with a strained smile, switching to English. "Why are you looking at me like that?"

Tina reached down, grabbed her by the arm, and pulled her out of the chair. "C'mon," she ordered in a no-nonsense manner. "You're coming with me and Beatrice, and we're going to Pete's for a slice."

Vilma tried to pull away, but her friend held her arm fast. "Look, Tina," she began. "I really don't feel like . . ." But then she noticed the expression on her friend's face. There was concern, genuine worry.

"C'mon, Vilma," Tina said, letting go of her arm. "We haven't talked in days. It'll do you good. It's gorgeous outside, and Beatrice has promised not to talk about how fat she's getting."

Vilma chuckled. It felt kind of good to laugh with someone, she realized.

"Let's go," Tina said, holding out her hand.

Tina was right, Vilma knew, and with a heavy sigh she took her friend's hand and followed her outside to catch up with Beatrice. It would be nice to get out with her friends. She needed a distraction.

The three girls headed down the driveway toward Pete's. Tina regaled them with tales about how her mother had threatened to throw her out of the house if she even thought about getting a belly button ring, and Beatrice, true to form, talked about her expanding bottom.

But Vilma was lost in thoughts of her own. She thought about how nice the weather was, now that spring had finally decided to show, and wondered if the sun was shining as brightly wherever Aaron Corbet was—and if it wasn't, she wished him sunshine.

Inside the cave, Mufgar of the Orisha clan squatted on bony legs and removed four pumice rocks from a leather pouch at his side. The diminutive creature with leathery skin the color of a dirty penny stacked the stones and, with the help of his three brethren, coaxed the remembrance of fire from the rocks.

The volcanic stones began to smolder, then glow an angry red as the four murmured a spell used by their kind for more than a millennia. Mufgar laid a handful of dried grass atop the rocks, and it immediately burst into flame. Shokad added some twigs to feed the hungry fire as Zawar and Tehom gathered their weapons and placed them against the cave wall until they were needed again.

The fire blazed warmly, and Mufgar adjusted his chieftain's headdress, which was made from the skull of a beaver and the pelts of two red foxes, upon his overly large, misshapen head.

Sitting down before the roaring campfire, he raised his long, spindly arms to the cave ceiling.

"Mufgar of the Orisha clan has called this council, and you have answered," he growled in the guttural tongue of his people. He leaned toward the fire and spit into the flames. The viscous saliva popped and sputtered as it landed on the burning twigs. "Blessed be they who are the Powers, those who allow us to experience the joys of living even though we have no right to this gift."

The three others cleared their throats and, one after the other, spewed into the blaze. "Praise be for the mercy of the Powers," the Orishas said in unison.

"We are as one," Mufgar said as he brought his arms down. "The council is seated. It has begun."

Mufgar gazed at the three who had gathered for this calling, saddened by how their numbers had dwindled over the centuries. He remembered a time when a cave of this size wouldn't have begun to hold the clan's numbers. Now, that was but a distant memory.

"I have called this council, for our merciful masters have bestowed upon us a perilous task," Mufgar said, addressing his followers. "A task with a most generous reward, if we should succeed." He looked at what remained of his tribe and saw the fear in their eyes—the same fear he felt deep within his own heart.

Shokad, the shaman, shook his head. His

long, braided hair, adorned with the small bones of many a woodling creature, rattled like chimes touched by the wind. He murmured something inaudible beneath his breath.

"Does something trouble you, wise Shokad?" Mufgar asked.

The old Orisha ran a bony hand across his wide mouth and gazed into the crackling fire. "I have been having troubling dreams of late," he replied, the small, dark wings on his back fluttering to life. "Dreams that show a place of great beauty, a place where all our kind have gathered and we live not under the yoke of the Powers," he whispered, making cautious reference to the host of angels that were their masters.

Mufgar nodded his skull-adorned head. "Your dreams show a future most interesting," he observed, stroking the long braid hanging from his chin. "If we succeed in our new task, our masters say they will reward us with blessed freedom. Our independence we will have earned."

"But . . . but to achieve this we must hunt the Nephilim," Tehom stammered. "Capture it and bring it to Verchiel." The great hunter looked as though he would break into tears, he was so filled with fright.

"If we wish to be free of the Powers," Mufgar said to them all, "we must complete this sacred chore. Then, and only then, will we be allowed to search for the Safe Place."

With the mention of the Orishas' most sacred

destination, all four blessed themselves by touching the center of their foreheads, the tips of their pointed noses, their mouths, and then their chests.

Zawar climbed to his feet, frantically dancing from one bare foot to the other. His wings fluttered nervously. "But our task is impossible," he said, pulling at the long, stringy hair on his head. "The Nephilim will destroy us with ease—look at how he bested the great Verchiel in combat. You saw the scars—we all saw the scars."

Mufgar remembered the burns covering Verchiel's body. The scars were severe, showing great anger and strength in the one who inflicted them. If that could be done to the one who was the leader of the Powers, what chance did they have? "It is the task bestowed upon us," he said with the authority that made him chief. "There is no other way."

"No," Shokad interjected, slowly shaking his head from side to side. "That is not true. The dreams show me a world where our masters have been destroyed by the Nephilim."

Mufgar felt himself grow more fearful. The shaman's dreams were seldom wrong, but what he was speaking—it went against the ways of the Orishas. Since their creation, they had served the Powers.

"You speak blasphemy," the leader hissed as he pointed a long, gnarled finger at the shaman. "It would not surprise me if Lord Verchiel himself appeared in this very cave and turned you to ash."

Tehom and Zawar huddled closer together, their large eyes scanning the darkness for signs of the terrifying angel's sudden arrival.

Shokad fed the fire with another handful of sticks. "I speak only of what I see in the ether," he said, moving his hand around in the air. "There is a new time coming, the dreams tell me. We need only pay attention."

It's tempting to embrace these new ideas, Mufgar thought, *to push aside the old ways and think of only the new.* But during his long life on this planet, he had seen the wrath of the Powers firsthand, and did not care to risk having it directed toward him.

"I will hear no more of this madness," Mufgar declared, his voice booming with power. "Our service to the masters is what has kept us alive."

Zawar climbed to his feet and went to their belongings stashed across the cave against the wall. "We live only as long as the Powers allow us to," he said, searching for something amongst their supplies. Finding it, he returned to the fire, where he sat down and opened the small bundle. Inside were the shriveled remains of dried field mice and moles. "When they no longer have need of our skills, they will destroy us, as they did our creators," Zawar said as he picked up a mouse and bit off its head for emphasis. He offered the snacks to the others.

Mufgar could not believe his ears. Had they

all been stricken with madness? *How can they speak such treason?* he wondered. But deep down he knew. The Powers had no love for them, thinking they were no better than animals. "Our creators broke the laws of God by making us," Mufgar explained in an attempt to restore their sanity with a reminder of their people's history. "We are blemishes upon the one God's world. The Powers have allowed us to live—to prove ourselves worthy of the life bestowed upon us by their fallen brethren. When we have done this, then and only then will we be given our freedom and allowed to search for the Safe Place."

Again, the Orishas blessed themselves.

"But what of the others of our clan?" Tehom asked, taking a stiffened mole from their rations. "What of those who defied our masters and went to find our most prized paradise?"

Mufgar did not want to hear this. No matter how he himself felt, to question the old ways would certainly bring about their doom. He remembered how he had tried to convince the others to stay, all the time wishing that he had had the courage to go with them. But he was chief, and was slave to the traditions of old.

Mufgar crossed his arms and puffed out his chest. "They are dead," he said definitely. "They have disobeyed our laws."

The shaman looked to Zawar and Tehom, who were both chewing their meal of dried vermin, then back to Mufgar. "But what if they aren't dead?" he asked in a clandestine whisper. "What if they succeeded in finding the paradise for which we so yearn? Think of it, Mufgar—think of it."

The chief stared into the fire, pondering the words of the shaman. *Could it have always been this simple? To steal away unnoticed and find their own Heaven.* "Lord Verchiel has said that any who defy his wishes would be expunged from existence."

Shokad slid closer. "But times are changing, Great Mufgar," he said. "Verchiel and his Powers are distracted by the prophecy."

"The Nephilim," Tehom said in a whisper, spitting fragments of dried mole into the fire.

Zawar, sitting next to him, nodded and flapped his wings. "It is said that he will bring forgiveness to the fallen." He picked a piece of tail from between his two front teeth. "And our masters do not want this, I think."

It had been hours since he'd last fed, and Mufgar snatched up a dried carcass from the open pouch. "So you suggest we disobey the Powers, ignore our orders—forsake our chance at true freedom." He took a bite of the mouse's head and waited for an answer. The dried meat had very little flavor, and he yearned for his favorite meal. It had been quite some time since he had feasted upon the delectable flesh of canine. Mouse and mole were fine for a time—but the meat of dog was something that he often dreamed of when his empty belly howled to be filled.

"A great conflict is coming between our masters and the Nephilim," the holy man proclaimed, "and only one will survive. The Nephilim's power is great. To attack him would invite our downfall."

Zawar and Tehom nodded in agreement. "Let the Nephilim destroy the Powers," Zewar said.

"And then we will be free," Tehom added.

Mufgar swallowed the last of his snack and climbed to his feet. He had heard enough. It was time to pass judgment. He raised his arms above his head again, gazing at the fire and his followers around it. "I, Mufgar, chief of the Deheboryn Orisha, have listened to the words of my clan and have applied my great wisdom to their concerns."

In his mind's eye he saw an image of those who had left the clan in search of the Safe Place. He saw them living in the beauty of Paradise— but then a dark cloud passed over, and from the sky, fire rained down upon them. The Nephilim had not defeated the Powers, and for their betrayal of the old ways, the Orishas were destroyed forever.

"We will continue to hunt the Nephilim," Mufgar said, avoiding the disappointed looks in his followers' eyes. "It is the only way I can guarantee the continued existence of our kind.

We will track the enemy of our masters and capture him—when we succeed, then we shall be
set free." Mufgar lowered his arms. "I have spoken," he said with finality. "This council is
ended." He turned from the fire and headed for
a darkened part of the cave where he would rest
before resuming the hunt.

"You doom us all," he heard Shokad say to
his back.

Mufgar reached for the dagger of bone tied
to his leg and leaped into the air, his wings carrying him over the fire. He landed upon the
shaman, knocking him back to the floor. Zawar
squealed with fear as Mufgar placed the knife
against the old Orisha's throat.

"I will hear no more of your blasphemous
talk," Mufgar said, gazing into Shokad's fear-
filled eyes. He pricked the leathery skin of the
oldster's throat with the tip of the dagger, drawing a bead of blood. "And if I do, the Nephilim
will not have his chance at you—for you will
have already doomed yourself."

Mufgar sheathed his blade and left the
shaman and the others cowering by the dwindling fire. Alone, curled into a tight ball on the
floor of the cave, the chief chased elusive sleep.
Finally he found it as the fire burned down, the
stones forgetting their past, leaving the cave in
darkness.

chapter two

Gabriel's tail wagged crazily as Aaron approached the picnic table at the back of the roadside restaurant.

"That's our lunch, isn't it, Aaron?" the dog said happily, his back end swaying from side to side with the force of his muscular tail. *"It sure smells good,"* he said with a heavy pant, sniffing at the bottom of the bags Aaron carried. *"I'm so hungry, I could eat cat food."*

Aaron laughed as he set the bags down on the wooden table. "Was that a joke, Gabe?" he asked the excited dog.

"No," the dog replied, his eyes never leaving the white bags. *"I really would eat cat food."*

Aaron laughed again and began to remove the food from the bags. Camael was sitting on one of the wooden benches gazing off into space, as if he was watching something a thousand miles away. For all Aaron knew, that very well could have been what he was doing.

"Did he give you a hard time while I was gone?" Aaron asked Camael. For some reason, Gabriel had not taken to the angel and was prone to being difficult when Aaron was not around.

"He chattered, but I ignored him," Camael said without turning. "And he did eat something off the ground, a filthy habit."

Aaron glanced down at the dog sitting obediently at his feet. "You know you're not supposed to do that," he said sternly.

Gabriel wagged his tail some more. *"It was gum,"* he said, as if that would make it all right.

"I don't care," Aaron said, picking up one of the wrapped sandwiches. "You could get sick."

"But I like gum."

Aaron squatted down in front of the dog and began to unwrap the burger. "Gum isn't for dogs. No gum. Get it?"

The Lab ignored him, instead sticking his snout inside the sandwich wrapper to see what Aaron held. *"Is this for me? Is this my lunch?"*

"Yep, it is," Aaron answered as he removed the meat from the bun. "You don't need any bread, though." He discarded the roll into one of the now empty bags.

"Hey, what are you doing that for?" Gabriel panicked. *"That's my lunch, you said. Why are you throwing it away?"*

Aaron held out the hamburger. "Here, this is what you want. I just threw away the bread. It'll make you fat."

Gabriel couldn't stop looking at the bag. *"But I want the bread, too,"* he whined pathetically.

Aaron sighed and shook his head. At first it had been fun being able to communicate with his best friend, but now he found it more and more like dealing with a small child. "Look, are you going to eat this or not?" he asked. "Usually you don't even have lunch, so this should be a treat."

The dog reluctantly pried his gaze from the bag and gently snatched the burger from Aaron's hand. He chewed once and then swallowed with a loud gulp.

Aaron patted the dog's side. "That was pretty good, huh?"

Gabriel licked his lips and gazed into his master's eyes. *"Any more?"*

"No," Aaron said. "I bought one for me and one for you. That's it."

"Are you going to eat your bread?" Gabriel asked

"Yes, I'm going to eat my bread."

"It will make you fat."

"You're too much, Gabriel." Aaron laughed. He took a bottle of water and poured some into a paper cup. "Here's some water to wash down your burger," he said as he set the cup on the ground in front of the dog.

Gabriel began to lap at the cup, careful not to tip it over. *"I'm still hungry,"* he grumbled between laps.

"Sorry," Aaron said, picking up his own burger and sitting down beside Camael. "Think of how good your supper will taste."

The dog grunted and strolled off to sniff at an overgrown patch of grass near the edge of the parking lot.

Aaron watched him go. He hated to be mean, but if he allowed Gabriel to eat every time he said he was hungry, the dog would weigh three hundred pounds. He couldn't begin to count all the overweight Labs he'd seen while working at the veterinary clinic back in Lynn, Massachusetts. It was the Labrador retriever curse—they loved to eat.

He sighed as he picked up his burger and took a bite. It was good, cooked just the way he liked it, medium rare, with lettuce, tomato, and a little mayo. He chewed for a moment, swallowed, and turned to Camael, still sitting silently and staring off into space. "What exactly are you looking at?"

"I see a great deal," the angel replied, his voice like a far-off rumble of thunder. "A father and son fishing by a stream, an old woman hanging laundry in her yard, a female fox teaching her litter how to hunt frogs." He paused, tilting his head as if to examine something at another angle. "It is what I do not see that interests me."

Aaron opened another bottle of water and took a sip. "Okay, what don't you see?"

"As of now, I see no sign of pursuit."

"And that's a good thing—right?" Aaron took another bite of his burger and reached for a cardboard container of French fries. He dumped half on the wrapper with the remains of his burger and placed the container with the rest in front of Camael.

The action broke the angel's steely stare, and he looked down on the container before him. "I told you, I do not need to eat," he said with a hint of a scowl.

Aaron bit half of a large fry and chewed. "You don't *need* to," he said. "Doesn't mean that you *can't*. Try one."

Camael slowly placed his hands on either side of the container. "As I was saying," he said, studying the French fries as if they were new forms of life, "I have seen no trace of the Powers since leaving your city of Lynn, so it would appear that the magickal wards I left to mask our passing have proven beneficial."

"Is that what you've been doing?" Aaron asked with surprise. He consumed the last bite of his burger. "I was a little worried by how slow we've been moving. I thought you were getting a little wrapped up in the whole sight-seeing thing."

Camael removed a French fry from the container and glared at it. "I have been on this planet for thousands of years, boy. The urge to 'sight-see' was purged long ago."

And then the angel did something that Aaron imagined he'd never see. Camael popped the French fry into his mouth and began to chew. He chewed for what seemed an insane amount of time and then swallowed. "Adequate," he said, tilting the container toward him and reaching for another.

Aaron took a sip of his water and smacked his lips. "Do you think these wards will be enough?" he asked. "I mean, will it keep them off our backs until we can find where they're keeping Stevie?"

The angel was eating fries like a pro, three and four at a time. *For someone who doesn't need to eat, he certainly seems to be enjoying himself,* Aaron thought as he waited for an answer.

"The wards are merely a distraction. My magickal skills are nowhere near Verchiel's and the Archons in his service—"

"Archons?" Aaron interrupted.

"Angels of the Powers who have mastered the complexities of angelic magick. They will see through our ruse sooner rather than later, but let us hope the wards will buy us enough time to find that to which you are being drawn."

Aaron had felt the strange sensation since leaving Lynn behind. He still didn't understand what it was—it seemed to be an urge, a need to travel north. Through New Hampshire, Vermont, and now Maine, he was being drawn inexorably northward. Even as he sat, finishing his lunch, he could feel it pulsing in his mind, urging him onward. "Do you think what I'm feeling will take us to Stevie?" he asked with hope.

Camael had finished the last of the fries, tipping over the container to be sure it was empty. "Your abilities are still young, Aaron. They are as much a mystery to me as they are to you."

"But it's possible, right?" he persisted. "Like maybe I'm somehow connected to Stevie—and I'm being drawn to him."

The angel nodded slowly. "It is possible," he said, his large hand stroking his silvery gray goatee. "But it may be that you are being pulled to something else—something of greater importance."

"I don't understand." Aaron stared intently at the angel. "What could I be drawn to if not Stevie? What can be more important than him?"

The angel remained silent, continuing to stroke his bearded chin, seemingly lost within his own thoughts.

"Camael?" Aaron prompted, raising his voice slightly.

"It is a most elusive place," Camael finally answered, his eyes glazed. Then he turned to Aaron and fixed him in an intense glare. "*Aerie*," he whispered. "You could be taking us to Aerie."

Faces flashed before Camael's eyes; images of those he'd saved from the destructive wrath of the Powers throughout the innumerable centuries since he'd left the angelic Host. *Where had they gone?* It was a question he often asked himself. Some were eliminated later, the Powers eventually tracking them and succeeding in their malevolent goals. But there were others, others who had managed to find a very special place, a place that still eluded him.

"Aerie?" Aaron was asking. "Isn't that a bird's nest or something?"

"It is a place unlike any other on this world, Aaron, a special place—a secret place, where those who have fallen await their reunion with Heaven." Camael folded his hands before him, remembering the times when he thought he had found it—only to be sadly disappointed.

"Have you ever been to this place?" the Nephilim asked.

"No. Aerie is hidden from me, for I am not fully trusted," he replied. "Remember, I was once the leader of the Powers, and they would like nothing more than to burn away Aerie and all it stands for."

"Are you sure there really is such a place?" Aaron asked.

Camael tried to imagine what his existence would have been like without the idea of Aerie's presence to comfort him. He doubted he would have been able to continue his mission without the promise of something better awaiting those he struggled to save—something better for himself. "It exists," he said quietly. "I'm sure of it—just as I know that you are of whom the prophecy speaks. And Aaron, those who live there, in this secret place, *they* believe in the prophecy that you personify." He paused. "They're waiting for you, boy."

Aaron seemed taken aback by this latest revelation. In a way, Camael felt pity for the youth and his human perceptions of the world. The idea of what he actually was, and what his true purpose was to be, must have been quite overwhelming for his primitive mind. Although he did have to admit that, at this moment, the youth wasn't doing too badly.

"All the people in Aerie—they're waiting for me to do for them what I did for Zeke?"

Camael nodded, remembering the valiant Grigori, who had helped him rescue Aaron during the Powers' attack on the boy's home. Zeke had been mortally wounded and the Nephilim had used his prophetic gift to forgive his trespasses and allow his return to Heaven. "It is your destiny to release *all* who repent," he said.

Aaron seemed to be digesting his words, the importance of his destiny sinking in even deeper. "Before I do any more forgiving, we're going to find Stevie," he said. "Wherever this urge is taking us, whether it's to my brother, or to Aerie, or to a place that makes really great tacos, finding Stevie and getting him away from that bastard Verchiel is the number one priority—agreed?"

Aaron demanded, an intense seriousness in his look.

Camael thought about arguing with the youth, but he sensed that it would be for naught. No matter how different Aaron Corbet had become since awakening the angelic power that resided within him, he still thought of himself as human. "Agreed," he answered.

There was still much Aaron had to learn—but that would come over time.

"That wasn't very nice," Gabriel grumbled as he sniffed along the grounds of the picnic area. *"Not very nice at all."*

He was following a scent, something that made his stomach growl and his mouth salivate. Gabriel was hungry—although there was seldom a time that he wasn't feeling the pangs of hunger. At a green trash barrel, he found the crumpled remains of an ice-cream sandwich wrapper. There were other pieces of trash that had missed the receptacle as well, but he would investigate those later, after he'd given the wrapper his full attention.

The dog was hurt that Aaron could be so insensitive to his needs. He was hungry, and Aaron still would not let him have the bread that he was going to throw away, anyway. It was frustrating and only served to make him hungrier.

Gabriel nudged the wrapper with his nose, pulling the delicious scents of dried vanilla ice cream and chocolate cookie up into his sensitive nostrils. His tongue shot out to lap at the wrapper, the moisture making the scents clinging to the refuse all the more pungent.

You don't eat things off the ground, he remembered Aaron scolding him. And he knew that he shouldn't, but he was angry, and so very hungry. Gabriel took the ice-cream sandwich wrapper into his mouth and began to chew. It didn't taste like much, but then, dogs don't have taste buds. The deliciousness of something was based entirely on its smell. If it smelled like something to eat, that was good enough for a dog, especially a Labrador. Very few things required more than a chew or two, and the paper wrapper was soon sliding down Gabriel's throat and into his stomach.

Unsatisfied and a little guilty, Gabriel turned his attention away from the barrel and toward a family of three who were having lunch at another of the picnic tables. The dog approached them, tail wagging in happy greeting. There were two adults, a mother and a father, and a little girl who was about the same age as Stevie.

A wave of sadness passed over the animal as he viewed the family. He missed the other members of his own pack; Tom and Lori were dead, and the Powers had taken Stevie away. But at least he still had Aaron. It wasn't how it used to be, but it would do for now. He still wasn't sure about the one called Camael. There was something about him that he didn't quite trust. He smelled too much like that nasty Verchiel to be accepted by him into the pack.

"Hello, doggie!" the little girl squealed as she turned on the bench and caught sight of him.

Gabriel could smell the caution seep from her parents' pores as he approached. He took no offense; after all, he was a strange dog and there were many that he himself would have been cautious of. He sat down, as Aaron had taught him, brought one of his paws up in greeting, barked softly once, and wagged his tail.

The little girl laughed happily, and he noticed the adults smile as well.

"May I pet him?" the child asked, already sliding off the bench.

"Let him smell you first, Lily," the father said cautiously. "You don't want to scare him."

The child held out her hand, and Gabriel sniffed the pink skin of her palm. Fragments of scents clung to her flesh: soap that smelled like bubble gum; cheese crackers; sugary fruit juice; her mother's perfume. Gently, he lapped the child's hand.

Lily squealed with delight and began to pat his head. "You're a good dog, aren't you," she cooed, "and your ears are so soft."

Gabriel already knew that, but it didn't prevent him from enjoying the child's attentions, until he caught the delicious aroma of food. He lifted his snout and pulled in the olfactory delights as he watched Lily's mother place a hot dog on the table where the child had been sitting.

"C'mon, Lily. Let the doggie go back to his family and you eat your lunch."

Lily patted his head again and leaned in very close. "Good-bye, doggie," she said, kissing his nose as his stomach gurgled loudly. "Was that your belly?" She giggled.

Gabriel looked deeply into her eyes. *"Yes,"* he answered with a short, grumbling bark.

She couldn't understand him as Aaron did, but still, she seemed to grasp his answer—as if he were somehow able to touch her mind.

"Are you hungry?" she asked.

Gabriel could not lie to the child and barked affirmatively while he used his mind to tell her that he would love a bite of her lunch.

The child suddenly turned and walked toward the picnic table. She snatched up her hot dog, tore off a hunk—bread and all—and brought it back to Gabriel.

"I don't know if you should do that, honey," her father cautioned.

Lily presented the food to the Lab, and he gently plucked it from her hand, swallowing it in one gulp. *Thank you, Lily,* he thought, looking into her eyes.

"You're welcome," she responded with a pretty smile.

Lily's father walked over, carrying his own sandwich in one hand. "Okay," he said, trying to steer the child back toward the table. "I think the doggie's had enough. Say good-bye now."

Gabriel stared intently at the man. *"Before I go,"* he directed his thoughts toward Lily's father, *"can I have a bite of your sandwich?"*

Without a moment's hesitation, the man tore off a piece of his hamburger and tossed it to the Lab.

Gabriel was satisfied. The painful pangs of his empty belly had been temporarily assuaged with the help of Lily and her parents—it had been awfully generous of them to share their lunch—and he was heading back to join Aaron, exploring as he went.

The tinkling of a chain was the first thing to capture his attention, and then he became aware of her scent.

Gabriel stopped at the beginning of an overgrown path that led to a small area designated for children. He noticed some swings, a tiny slide, and a wooden playhouse shaped like a train. Again came the jangle of a chain, and from behind the playhouse appeared another dog, her nose pressed to the sand as she followed a scent that had caught her fancy.

Gabriel's tail began to wag furiously as he padded down the path and barked a friendly greeting. *How good is this?* he thought. *A full belly and now somebody to play with.*

The female flinched, startled by his approach. Her tail wagged cautiously. She, too, was a yellow Labrador retriever and she wore a pretty, red bandanna around her neck, as well as the chain.

43

He moved closer. *"I'm Gabriel."*

The female continued to stare, and he noticed that the hackles of fur at the back of her neck had begun to rise.

"Don't be afraid," he said soothingly. *"I just want to play."* He lay down on the ground to show her that he meant no harm. *"What's your name?"*

The female moved slowly toward him, sniffing at the air, searching for signs of a threat. *How odd,* thought Gabriel. *Maybe her family doesn't let her play with other dogs.* *"I'm Gabriel,"* he said again.

"Tobi," she replied, hackles still raised.

"Hello, Tobi. Do you want to chase me?" he asked pleasantly, rising to all fours.

Tobi sniffed at him again and growled nervously. Slowly, she began to back away, her tail bending between her legs.

Gabriel was confused. *"What's the matter?"* he asked, advancing toward her. *"You don't have to chase me if you don't want to—I could chase you instead."*

Tobi snapped at him with a bark, her lips peeled back in a fierce snarl as she continued to back toward the playhouse.

Gabriel stopped. *"What's wrong?"* he asked, genuinely concerned and quite disappointed. *"Why won't you play with me?"*

"Not dog," Tobi growled as she sniffed the air around him. *"Different,"* she spat, and fled around the playhouse in the direction she'd come.

Gabriel was stunned. At first, he had no idea

what Tobi meant, but then he thought of that day when he had almost died. He flinched, remembering the intensity of the pain he had felt when the car struck him. Aaron had done something to him that day, had laid his hands upon him and made the pain go away. That was the day everything became clearer.

The day he became different?

He left the play area, his mind considering the idea that he might not be a dog anymore, when he heard Aaron call. Gabriel quickened his pace and joined his friend and Camael. They were cleaning up their trash and getting ready to resume their journey.

"Where've you been?" Aaron asked as they headed toward the parking lot.

"*Around,*" Gabriel replied, not feeling much like talking.

A car on its way out of the lot passed them as they waited to cross to their own vehicle. In the back, he saw Tobi staring intently at him. It wasn't only the window glass that separated him from her, he thought sadly as he watched the car head down the road.

"Are you all right?" Aaron asked as he bent to scratch under the dog's chin.

"*I'm fine,*" Gabriel answered, unsure of his own words—recalling the truth revealed in another's.

"*Not dog. Different.*"

interlude one

"This will sting, my liege."

Verchiel hissed with displeasure as the healer laid a dripping cloth on the mottled skin of his bare arm.

"Why do I not heal, Kraus?" the leader of the Powers asked.

The blind man patted down the saturated material and reached for another patch of cloth soaking in a wooden bowl of healing oil, made from plants extinct since Cain took the life of his brother, Abel. "It is not my place to say, my lord," he said, his unseeing eyes glistening white in the faint light streaming through the skylight of the old classroom.

The abandoned school on the grounds of the Saint Athanasius Church, in western Massachusetts, had been the Powers' home since the battle with the Nephilim. This was where they plotted—

awaiting the opportunity to continue their war against those who would question their authority upon the world of God's man.

Verchiel shifted uncomfortably in the high-backed wooden chair, stolen from the church next door, as the healer laid yet another cloth upon his burn-scarred flesh. "Then answer me this: Do these wounds resemble injuries sustained in a freak act of nature, or do they bear the signature of a more divine influence?"

He was trying to isolate the cause of the intense agony that had been his constant companion since he was struck by lightning during his battle with Aaron Corbet. The angel wanted to push the pain aside, to box it up and place it far away. But the pain would not leave him. It stayed, a reminder that he might have offended his Creator—and was being punished for his insolence.

"It is my job to heal, Great Verchiel," Kraus said. "I would not presume to—"

Verchiel suddenly sprang up from his seat, the heavy wooden chair flipping backward as his wings unfurled to their awesome span. Kraus stumbled as winds stirred by the angel's wings pushed against him.

"I grant you permission, ape," the angel growled over the pounding clamor caused by the flapping of his wings. "Tell me what you feel in your primitive heart." His hands touched the scars upon his chest as he spoke. "Tell me if you believe it was the hand of God that touched me in this way!"

"Mercy, my master!" Kraus cried, cowering upon the floor. "I am but a lowly servant. Please do not make me think of such things!"

"I will tell you, Verchiel," said a voice from across the room.

Verchiel slowly turned his attention to a dark corner of the classroom, where a large cage of iron was hanging from the ceiling, its bars etched with arcane markings. It swayed in the turbulence caused by his anger. The stranger taken from the monastery in the Serbian Mountains peered out from between the iron bars, the expression on his gaunt face intense.

"Do you care to hear what I have to say?" he asked, his voice a dry whisper.

"Ah, our prisoner is awake," Verchiel said. "I thought the injuries inflicted by my soldiers would have kept you down for far longer than this."

The prisoner clutched the bars of his cage with dirty hands. "I've endured worse," he said. "Sometimes it is the price one must pay."

Verchiel's wings closed, retracting beneath the flesh of his bare back. "Indeed," the angel snarled.

Kraus still cowered upon the floor, head bowed. "You will leave me now," Verchiel said, dismissing the human healer. "Take your things and go."

"Yes, my lord," the blind man said, gathering up the satchel containing his tools of healing and carefully feeling his way to the exit.

"Why do they do it?" the prisoner asked as he watched the healer depart. "What perverse need is satisfied by the degradation we heap upon them? It's a question I've gone round and round with for years."

"Perhaps we give their mundane lives purpose," Verchiel responded, advancing toward the cage. "Providing them with something that was lacking when they lived among their own kind." Verchiel stopped before the hanging cage and gazed into the eyes of his prisoner. "Or maybe they are just not as intelligent as we think," he said with perverse amusement.

"And that's reason enough to exploit and abuse them?" the prisoner asked.

"So be it, if it serves a greater good. They are aiding us in carrying out God's will. They are serving their Creator—as well as ours. Can you not think of a more fulfilling purpose?"

Still dressed in the tattered brown robes of the Serbian monastery, the prisoner sat down with a smile, leaning back against the bars of the cage. "And you seriously have to wonder what it was that struck you down?" He chuckled, making reference to Verchiel's scars. "Wouldn't think you were that dense, but then again . . ."

Verchiel loomed closer, peering through the black iron bars. "Please share with me your thoughts," he whispered. "I'm eager to hear the perceptions of one such as you—the most renowned of the fallen. Yes, please, what is the Lord God thinking these days?"

The prisoner casually reached within his robes and withdrew the mouse. Gently, he touched the top of its pointed head with the tip of his finger as it crawled about on his open palm. "That I couldn't tell you, Verchiel," he said, looking up as the tiny creature scuttled up the front of his robe to his shoulder. "It's been quite some time since the Creator and I last spoke. But looking at your current condition, I'd have to guess that He's none too happy with you either."

And then the prisoner smiled—a smile filled with warmth and love, and so stunningly beautiful. How could he not have once been the most favored of God's children?

Verchiel felt his rage grow, and it took all the self-control he could muster to not reach into the cage and rend his captive limb from limb. "And I am to believe the likes of you"—the Powers' leader growled reaching out to clutch the bars of the cage—"the Prince of Lies?"

"Touché," the prisoner said, as the mouse explored the top of his head. "But remember," he said with a grin, "I *have* had some experience in these matters."

chapter three

Trudging through the wood, in search of his prey, Mufgar, chieftain of the Deheboryn Orisha, knew that his decision the previous night had been the right one.

With his primitive elemental magicks, Mufgar had coerced the dirt, rock, and stone of the tunnel system in which they traveled to alter its labyrinthian course and open a passageway to the surface. "We will never catch a scent down here," he had said to his party as the dirt face of a nearby wall became like a thing of liquid, swirling and falling away to reveal a newly fashioned tunnel that ascended to the surface. "It is on the land above where our destiny awaits us."

Mufgar had thanked the elements for their assistance, leaving an offering of dried fruit before beginning his ascension into the new morning sun. It had been eight hours since he and his tribe had emerged from below, eight hours since any had spoken a word to him.

He sensed their anger, their fear, and their disappointment over the judgment he had passed upon them. He was truly sorry that they questioned his decision, but he knew they would not abandon their duty to their masters. They would hunt the Nephilim as the Powers had ordered, capture him, and earn their freedom. *That is how it will be*, he thought, remembering the strange vision he'd had while sleeping. A vision of success.

Mufgar raised his hand to stop their progress through the dense wood. He listened carefully to sounds around him, the chirping of various birds, the rustling of the wind through trees heavy with leaves—and something else.

"Is it the Nephilim, Mufgar?" Tehom hissed at his side, raising his spear and looking nervously about the forest.

"No," the Orisha chieftain said. He listened again to the sounds way off in the distance, the sounds of machines. *What are they called?* He searched his brain for the strange-sounding word. *Automobiles*, he remembered with great satisfaction. "Not the Nephilim," he whispered, "but vehicles that will bring him to us."

Mufgar pointed through the woods to somewhere off in the distance. "I saw it in a vision of my own," he said, deciding to share his experience with his subjects, to give them faith in his

leadership. He turned and glared at Shokad. "As I slept, I, too, had a vision. A vision that the Nephilim would come to us—"

The shaman quickly looked away with a scowl upon his ancient features.

"—and he would fall against our might." Mufgar raised his spear in an attempt to rally his hunters. "And for our bravery, Lord Verchiel bestowed upon us our freedom, and we found the location of the blessed Safe Place."

The Orishas all bowed their malformed heads, blessing themselves furiously.

It had been the strangest dream, as clear as the day they hunted in now. It was all there for him, all the answers he had sought. The doubts he had been experiencing since the last council all dispelled like smoke in the wind. A holy vision had been bestowed upon him, maybe from the spirits of the great creators themselves, a vision that told him they would be victorious. He could ask for nothing better.

Mufgar turned to the shaman, who lagged behind. The old Orisha squatted down and took a handful of bones and smooth, shiny rocks from a purse at his side.

"You do not trust your chieftain's sleeping visions, Shokad?" he asked the shaman.

The old creature said nothing as he tossed the bones and stones onto the ground before him. His wings unfurled and fluttered nervously as he began to read the results of his throw.

"Hmmmm," he grumbled, rubbing his chin as he discerned the signs.

"What do they say, Shokad?" Mufgar asked. "Do the bones and stones speak of victory and freedom?"

The old Orisha was silent as he gathered up his tools of divination and returned them to his purse.

"Speak, shaman," Mufgar ordered. "Your chief commands you to reveal what you have seen."

"The bones and stones speak of death," Shokad said gravely.

Zawar and Tehom gasped beside him. "Death?" Tehom asked in a voice filled with dread.

"Death . . . but for whom?" Zewar wanted to know.

Shokad shook his head, the bones in his hair rattling as they struck one another. "They were not specific, but I can imagine no less for those who would go up against the might of the Nephilim." He glared at Mufgar, challenging his word as chief.

"But what of those who abandon the wishes of their masters?" Mufgar asked in return. "What is the fate of those who defy the Powers? Is the edict of that not death as well?"

The shaman scowled. "Possibly," he answered, "but it does not change the fact that death is our companion. We must choose our path wisely, or we may never have the opportunity to seek out the paradise that has long eluded us."

Zawar and Tehom glanced at each other, the conflicting messages of chief and shaman bringing the curse of dissension to their ranks.

"Great Mufgar," Zawar whispered as he looked about the woods, searching for any telltale signs of imminent death, "how do we choose?"

Mufgar looked back toward the sounds of the road in the distance. "There is only one choice," he said, moving away from them toward the road. "The hunt—and from that shall spring our freedom." He didn't even turn to see if they were following. Mufgar did not need to, for he knew that they were behind him.

He had seen it in his dream.

Aaron kept his speed at forty-five and continued down the winding, back road. He tightened his grip on the steering wheel as the excitement continued to build within him. They were getting closer to their destination, he could feel it thrumming in his body. "Is it just me, or do you feel this too?" he asked.

Camael grunted, staring at the twisting road before them.

"What?" Aaron said. "Do you see something?"

The angel remained silent, squinting as if trying to see more clearly ahead. Aaron couldn't take it anymore. The sensation he felt was akin to a guy with an orange flag at the finishing line. He was close—to what, he wasn't exactly sure, but his body was telling him that this is where they were supposed to be. "What do you see, for Christ's sake!" he yelled.

Camael slowly turned his attention from the windshield to the boy. His gaze was steely, cold.

"Sorry," Aaron said, attempting to squelch the feeling of unbridled excitement that coursed through his body. "It's just that I think we've found where they've taken Stevie—I'm excited. I didn't mean to yell at you."

The angel turned back to the road before them and pointed. "In the distance, not too far from here, I see a town."

Aaron waited a minute, but Camael offered no more. "That's it?" he asked impatiently. "That's all you see, a town?"

Gabriel, who had been in a deep, snoring sleep in the backseat, began to stir. In the rearview mirror, Aaron could see the Lab sit up, languidly licking his chops as he surveyed his surroundings.

"Where's the town?" the dog asked. *"All I see is woods."*

"Camael sees it in the distance," Aaron answered. "I've got a feeling that it might be where Verchiel has taken Stevie."

"There is something about this town," Camael said slowly, his eyes closed in concentration, his hand slowly stroking his silver goatee. "But I cannot discern what it is. It perplexes me."

Aaron reached over to the glove compartment and popped it open. The angel recoiled, but Aaron paid him little mind as he rummaged through the compartment while trying to keep his eyes on the road and the car in its lane. "What's it called? Maybe I can find it on the map," he said, slamming the glove compartment closed and shaking the map out in his lap.

"It is called Blithe," Camael said. "I believe the settlement would be considered quite old, by human standards."

"Is it even on here?" Aaron asked, dividing his attention between the map and the road. "I want to see how much farther we have to go—"

"Let's stop now," Gabriel suddenly said from the back.

"Let's see how far away Blithe is first," Aaron said as he glanced at the dog in the rearview mirror.

Gabriel seemed genuinely uncomfortable, climbing to all fours and pacing around the seat. *"I don't think I can wait,"* he said, a touch of panic in his voice.

Aaron was about to reply when the smell wafted up from the back. "Oh, my God," he said, and frantically rolled down his window.

"What are you doing?" Camael asked with his usual touch of petulance as the wind from the open window whipped at his hair. And then Aaron watched as the angel's expression turned from one of annoyance to one of absolute repulsion. "What is that smell?" he asked with a furious snarl.

With one hand over his nose and mouth, Aaron motioned over his shoulder to the sole inhabitant of the backseat.

The angel turned to face the dog. "What have you done?"

Gabriel simply stared out the back window.

"He's got gas," Aaron explained, his voice muffled by the hand still over his face. "It happens when he eats stuff he's not supposed to."

"It's vile," Camael said, glaring at the dog. "Something should be done so that it never happens again."

Aaron gazed into the rearview mirror. "What did you eat at that rest stop, Gabe?" he scolded, already knowing full well that the dog would have eaten anything.

Gabriel did not respond. Aaron didn't really expect him to. He pulled the car to the side of the road.

"What now?" Camael asked.

"There's only one way to deal with this problem," he said as he parked the car and got out. He opened the back door to let his friend out. "Maybe one of these days you'll learn not to eat everything in sight," he scolded the dog.

Gabriel jumped to the ground. *"I didn't eat everything—they still had plenty when I left."*

"Wait a minute," Aaron said, watching as the dog strolled away, snout firmly planted to the forest floor. "Who still had plenty? Did somebody give you food?"

"*I have to do my business,*" Gabriel said, eluding his master's question and moving deeper into the woods.

"What's the matter with right here?" Aaron asked, exasperated. "Gabriel, we have to get going."

"*I can't go if you're watching me,*" he heard the dog say before disappearing around a cluster of birch trees.

"When did you become so freakin' modest?" Aaron muttered beneath his breath. "Probably happened when I brought you back from the dead." He walked to the front of the car where Camael stood looking up the road. "So what do you think?" he asked the angel. "What are we going to find in Blithe?"

Camael shook his head slowly. "I honestly do not know."

Aaron crossed his arms and gazed at the road ahead. "The way I'm feeling right now, I'd have to say it's definitely something interesting."

"I will certainly agree with that," Camael said. He tilted back his head and sniffed at the air.

Aaron watched him grow suddenly tense and look about them cautiously. "What's wrong?"

"Do you not smell it?" he asked.

Aaron sniffed the air. He could smell nothing except the spring forest in full bloom. "I can't smell anything but the woods . . ." he began, and then he caught a whiff of it. It was a musky scent, an animal smell, but one he did not recognize. "What is it?"

Camael held out his hand, and Aaron watched as a spark of orange flame appeared and grew into a sword of fire.

"Orishas," the angel growled.

Aaron was about to ask what an Orisha was, when Gabriel's barks of fear ripped through the quiet stillness of the woods beyond, like a staccato burst of gunfire. "Gabriel," he cried, a fire sword of his own sparking to life in his hand.

Aaron charged into the woods, his blade decimating saplings and low-hanging branches in his path. Camael was at his side when the two stopped abruptly at the edge of a clearing.

"What the hell are those things?" Aaron whispered in fearful wonder.

There were four in all; ugly creatures no more than three feet tall, with skin the color of tarnished copper. They appeared primitive, dressed in strips of leather and fur, their long, stringy hair adorned with bones. One wore a fancy headdress made from what looked like animal pelts. From their backs sprang small, black-feathered wings that fluttered noisily, like flapping window shades. They had thrown a makeshift net over Gabriel, and were attempting to subdue the struggling dog.

"Those are Orishas," Camael answered. "Crude attempts by my fallen brethren to create life."

"Not very successful, I'd gather?"

"Miserable failures that would have been

eradicated long ago if it weren't for the Powers. They use the Orishas as slaves, as hunter trackers."

"So they're not that dangerous—right?" Aaron asked as he watched the Orishas forced back by Gabriel's wild thrashing.

"On the contrary," Camael said. "They have proven quite ferocious in battle, despite their diminutive size."

Gabriel's blocky head emerged from beneath the netting, and he snapped at his attackers. *"Aaron, I could use some help!"* he hollered, catching sight of his friend.

The Orishas turned and began to stalk toward Aaron and Camael, snarling menacingly. Three snatched up crude spears from the forest floor, and the one with the headdress removed a dagger from a sheath on its bony leg.

Aaron tensed, holding his flaming weapon before him. "What do we do?" he asked the angel standing calmly beside him.

"The Powers have probably put a bounty on our heads," Camael said casually as if talking about the weather. "The Orishas will try to capture us, and if that is not possible, they will surely attempt to kill us."

The primitive creatures were closer, and Aaron could hear them growling, a high-pitched sound like an air conditioner in need of repair— only much more horrible. "What do we do?" he repeated frantically.

"I thought it obvious, boy," the angel said as

enormous wings of white languidly unfurled from his back. "We kill them."

"Something told me you were going to say that," Aaron said, just as the Orishas shrieked a cry of war and launched themselves at their chosen prey.

The power that resided within Aaron wanted out in the worst way. He could feel it pacing about inside, like a bored jungle cat in its cage at the zoo. It had started when Camael first mentioned the Orishas. Like asking Gabriel if he wanted to go for a ride, the power of the Nephilim had perked right up, pushing at the restraints he had imposed upon it.

The Orishas were taking flight, their small, ebony wings flapping with blurring speed, and the angelic power struggled harder to be free, but Aaron wouldn't allow it. In fact, just the thought of undergoing the transformation, as he had that horrible night in Lynn, made him tremble with fear. "You're lucky I'm even using one of these damned swords," he muttered to himself as he raised his burning weapon and swatted the first of his attackers from the air.

The creature shrieked in agony as it plummeted to the ground, one of its wings aflame. It began digging up clumps of cool dirt and rubbing it on its smoldering feathers as Aaron turned his attention to Camael.

Another Orisha was moving with blinding speed toward the angel—spear aimed at his face.

At the last second, the creature suddenly changed direction and thrust its shaft down into Camael's chest. With a great bellow of pain, the angel raised his sword and sliced the warrior creature in two.

"Aaron, look out!" Gabriel called from behind him.

Aaron quickly turned, just in time to block the attack of another of the horrible beasts. It was the one with the elaborate headdress.

"You will fall before our might," the chieftain shrieked in its savage tongue. *"I have foreseen it."*

Aaron swung his mighty sword, and the Orisha fluttered backward as the burning blade nearly severed his overly large head from its diminutive body. The power within Aaron was wild now, straining for release. The chief again pressed the attack, and this time his knife found its mark, sinking into the soft flesh of Aaron's shoulder. He cried out in pain as the creature hovered just out of reach.

"Aaron, are you all right?"

"I'm fine, Gabriel," he said as he watched the dog try to pin the fighting Orisha with the burned wing to the forest floor. "Just pay attention. These things are dangerous."

The wound pulsed painfully, and a strange, burning sensation began to spread down his arm, making it difficult to hold his weapon. *Poison?* he wondered. He turned to Camael just in time to watch the angel warrior fall to his knees.

"Did I mention that the Orishas dip their

blades in a narcotic that immobilizes their prey?" Camael asked, his speech slightly slurred.

"You don't say," Aaron replied with sarcasm, as the sword fell from his numbed hand, imploding to nothing before it could hit the forest floor.

No longer concerned with them, now that the drug was coursing through their veins, the surviving Orishas turned their attention to Gabriel. Aaron watched helplessly as his friend lost his grip on the creature with the burned wing and it scuttled over to join its comrades.

"Get out of there, Gabriel!"

The chief had retrieved the net, and the three warriors slowly advanced on the snarling dog.

"You should know by now that I won't leave you," the Lab growled, standing his ground.

"Loyal to a fault," Camael said as he swayed upon his knees and fell to his side, the Orishas' poison taking hold.

The Orishas threw themselves at Gabriel. Two grabbed hold of the snarling dog while the chieftain tossed the net over his head. Quickly, they staked the net to the ground, trapping the Labrador.

"We will eat hardy tonight, my brothers," the chief said excitedly as he leaned in to sniff at the still snarling animal. *"A meal befitting warriors— warriors who are about to receive their freedom and safe passage to paradise."*

The Orishas began to cheer, their poison-dipped weapons raised to the heavens in a dance of victory.

"They're going to eat Gabriel?" Aaron asked with horror. His entire body had gone numb, and he slumped to the ground near Camael.

"It appears that way," the angel managed. "And then they will bring us to Verchiel at first light."

"What are we going to do?" Aaron asked while keeping his eyes on the jubilant Orishas, who seemed to be getting quite a kick out of tormenting poor Gabriel.

"It is up to you," Camael calmly replied.

"What the hell is that supposed to mean?" Aaron angrily barked.

"You have the power. All you need to do is use it."

As if on cue, Aaron felt the presence surge within him once again. "I don't know what you mean," he lied, using all his might to hold it at bay.

"Don't play games with me, Aaron," the angel snapped. "I can sense how it struggles to exert itself. Set it free."

"I . . . I can't do that," Aaron replied, gripped by fear. "I don't know if I can control it."

"I thought we were beyond this." The angel sounded exasperated. "The power is part of you—it is what you are now."

Deep down, Aaron knew the angel was right—but it didn't make it any less scary. The force was wild, its potential for destruction great. He remembered how he had felt the night Verchiel killed his foster parents. Such strength, such power, it had been exhilarating—at first.

Am I strong enough? he wondered. *Or will it drive me crazy as it has others before me?*

"I . . . I can't," he stammered. It was becoming more difficult to speak.

"You must," Camael declared. "If you do not, Gabriel will die and we will share a fate at the hands of Verchiel."

Aaron was silent. He watched the Orisha chief step away from the celebration and remove two sets of restraints from a satchel hidden in the thick underbrush. *"When the Orishas' poison wears off, you will go nowhere,"* the ugly little creature cackled as he moved toward Aaron.

"Do something!" Camael bellowed.

For a moment, Aaron thought about letting the power loose, feeling the electric surge of his true supernatural nature course through his body. He remembered the excruciating pain as his newly developed wings tore through the flesh of his back, unfurling to their full and glorious span. He winced, recalling the severe, burning sensation as ancient angelic symbols appeared upon his skin—signaling his transformation into something far more than human.

He thought about it, but he did nothing—and the Orisha's restraints snapped coldly closed around his wrists.

Camael sighed. He'd had such great hopes for the boy, but now he was beginning to have doubts.

"And now you, great angel," the Orisha chieftain said happily as he headed for Camael with the second set of manacles.

"And now me," Camael growled, and began to climb to his feet.

"More poison! More poison!" the leader screamed in panic, pulling his knife from the sheath around his leg. The other two warriors made a frantic dive for their weapons.

Camael was both bored and immensely annoyed. The angel knew that Aaron had been holding back, fearful of his newly emerged nature, and he had seen this as the perfect opportunity for the boy to tame the power, to wrestle it beneath his control. But as he gazed at the youth, lying upon the ground, having succumbed to the effects of the Orishas' poison—he realized how wrong he was. He wasn't ready at all, and Camael began to fear for the fulfillment of the angelic prophecy.

The old shaman was fluttering in the air before Camael, muttering, arms spread wide. The ground beneath the angel's feet began to churn, and he felt himself pulled into the earth as suddenly as liquid. The other two Orishas charged, their weapons glinting with paralyzing poison. *This will not do at all*, the angel thought as a new sword of fire ignited in his hand. Camael swung the fiery blade driving back the warriors and with one great flap of his mighty wings, he lifted himself from the ground's sucking embrace.

With a howl of fury, the chieftain launched himself toward Camael, moving with supernatural speed. But Camael was faster, swinging his sword of fire and cleaving the leader in two.

"Your dream was just that," he said as the two pieces of the once living thing fell away in flames. "A dream."

Without his leader, the Orisha with the burned wings seemed to lose his urge to fight. The fluttering beast drew back his arm, threw his spear, and turned to run. Camael slapped the projectile away, then pointed the tip of his sword at the fleeing primitive. A tongue of flame snaked from the end of the burning blade, and in an instant the Orisha warrior was engulfed in heavenly fire. The creature squealed: words of prayer to some long-dead fallen angel that was its creator upon its lips as it was incinerated.

There is one more, Camael thought as he returned to the ground, wings folding upon his back. Sword ready, his birdlike eyes scanned the trees and underbrush for signs of the older Orisha, but the creature was nowhere to be found.

Aaron moaned in the grip of the poison-induced fever, and Camael turned his attention to the Nephilim. His sword dissipated as he moved toward the youth and squatted beside him. He touched the locking mechanism on Aaron's manacles and watched as the restraints fell smoldering to the ground. "Get up, boy," he said sternly.

Aaron's eyes fluttered open. "Camael?" he whispered. "How . . . ?"

"I purged the poison from my system," he said, grabbing the teen by the front of his shirt and hauling him to his feet. "It's something you could have done as well, if you'd bothered."

He swayed drunkenly. "Why . . . why did you wait so long?"

Camael strode toward Gabriel still trapped beneath the net. "I was waiting for you to act," the angel answered as he pulled the stakes from the ground.

Gabriel surged up and shook himself free of the net. *"Thank you, Camael."* He sniffed at one of the still burning corpses of the Orisha warriors.

"So this . . . this was some kind of test?" Aaron asked, stumbling toward them on legs still numb with toxin.

Gabriel nuzzled his friend's hand. *"Are you all right? I was very worried about you."*

Aaron absently patted the dog's head as he waited for Camael's answer.

"You handled yourself quite bravely against the Powers—but now comes the difficult part," the angel said. "I wanted to see what you would do."

"Don't you worry about me. I'll be ready to deal with Verchiel when the time comes."

Camael scowled and motioned to the Orisha bodies littering the ground. "These are merely pests in the grand scheme of things, bothersome insects that should have been swatted away easily."

"I'm still new to this," Aaron defended himself. "*I* have a hard time killing. There's a lot I need to learn before—"

"You do not have time," Camael interrupted. "Verchiel is like a wounded animal now—he will do everything and anything in his power to see you destroyed."

"*What's this?*" the angel heard Gabriel mutter. He glanced over to see the Lab sniffing at a patch of overturned dirt, his pink nose pressed to the ground, his furry brow wrinkled in concentration.

"I'll be ready," Aaron said bravely, distracting Camael from the dog's curiosity. "Don't worry about me."

"I hope you are right, Aaron Corbet," Camael said with caution. "For there is far more at stake here than just your life."

He was about to suggest that they continue on to Blithe when the Orisha shaman exploded from the earth in front of the dog, eyes bulging with madness, jagged teeth bared in a grin of savagery.

"*You will not keep me from the Safe Place!*" it screamed as it lunged at the startled animal.

The shaman grabbed hold of Gabriel's flank and bit down into the fur-covered flesh of his thigh. The dog yelped in agony, snapping at the creature as it scurried off into the protection of the forest, wiping the dog's blood from its mouth.

Camael and Aaron ran to their injured comrade.

"He bit me, Aaron," Gabriel whined pathetically. *"That wasn't very nice. I didn't even bite him first."*

"He's got a pretty good bite here," Aaron said as he examined the bloody puncture wounds near the dog's hip. "What am I going to do?" Aaron asked, looking to Camael for help.

"That's an excellent question," the angel answered, folding his arms across his broad chest. "What *are* you going to do?"

"Nothing's happening," Aaron said as he laid his hands on the dog's bleeding leg.

"Perhaps you're not trying hard enough," Camael responded in that condescending tone of voice that made Aaron want to tell him to stick it up his angelic butt.

He was still angry with the angel for putting their lives at risk just to test him—although part of him did understand why Camael had done it. After all, there was quite a bit riding on this whole angelic prophecy thing. If he was in fact the one the prophecy spoke of, and they were both pretty sure that he was, then he had a major responsibility to fulfill for the fallen angels living upon the planet.

"Yeah," Gabriel added, interrupting his thoughts. *"Try harder."*

"That's enough out of you," Aaron said, pressing his hands against the bite. If only he could remember what he did that awful morning in Lynn when Gabriel had been hit by the car. After all, if he could return him from the brink of death then, he could certainly heal a simple bite now.

"*It hurts, Aaron.*"

"I know, pal. I'm going to fix you up, just as soon as . . ."

Camael bent closer. "Let go of your humanity and embrace the angelic," he boomed. "To fear it is to fear yourself."

Aaron was reminded of similar words spoken by Zeke that fateful Saturday—*had it really only been two weeks ago? So much had changed in such a short time.* He closed his eyes and willed the power forward.

He could sense it there, somewhere in the pitch black behind his eyes. He beckoned to it, but it ignored his call, perhaps perturbed at him for not allowing it to manifest during the battle with the Orishas. He concentrated all the more, his body trembling with exertion.

"That's it, rein it in," he heard Camael say quietly from beside him. "Take control and make it your own."

Aaron commanded the power to come forward, and it slowly turned its attention to him. He pushed again with his mind, and suddenly, with the speed of thought, it moved, shifting its form—mammal, insect, reptile, all shapes of life, the menagerie of God. The force surged through him, and Aaron gasped with the rush of it. His eyes flew open, and he gazed up into the late afternoon sky, at the clouds above and the universe beyond his own. "It's here," he whispered, feeling his body throb with the ancient power.

"Excellent," Camael hissed in his ear. "Now wrestle it, take control—show it you are the master."

And Aaron did as he was told. The power fought him, trying to overwhelm him with the sheer force of its might, but Aaron held on, corralling it, moving its strength to where it was needed. He felt the power flood into his upper body, moving down the length of his arms and into his hands.

"*I . . . I feel something happening, Aaron,*" Gabriel said, fear in his guttural voice.

"It's going to be all right," Aaron soothed as he felt the raw energy flow from the tips of his fingers into the dog's injured leg. He willed the power to heal his best friend, and he stared at the gaping wound, waiting for it to close—but nothing happened. Again, he willed it, and the power danced about the injury—but it did nothing.

Aaron pulled away, exhausted, hands tingling painfully. "I don't understand," he said in a breathless whisper. He looked up at Camael looming above him. "I did what you said—I took control and I commanded it to heal Gabriel's wound—but it didn't do a thing."

Camael stared thoughtfully at the Lab, absently reaching up to run his fingers through his goatee. "Interesting," he observed. "Perhaps your animal has become more complex than even you understand."

Aaron shook his head, confused. "I don't . . ."

"When the animal was healed before—"

"This animal has a name," Gabriel interrupted with annoyance.

"It's okay, boy," Aaron said, patting the dog's head, comforting him.

"As I was saying," Camael said, glaring at the dog, "when the animal was healed before, the power you wielded was raw, in its purest form—its most potent state. You commanded it to repair Gabriel, and it did just that—only I think it may have altered him as well."

"I don't feel altered," the dog said. *"My leg just hurts."*

"Are you saying that Gabriel is too complicated a life-form for me to fix now?"

The angel nodded.

"But how could I have done that?" Aaron asked as he gently stroked his dog's side.

"You didn't," Camael corrected. "You just gave the command, and the presence within you took it from there."

If he hadn't been afraid of the power that lived within him before, he certainly would be now, but that didn't change the fact that Gabriel was still hurt. "Gabriel needs medical attention," Aaron said, staring down at his best friend. "He may be a complex life-form, but he still needs to have that bite cleaned up."

"Then I suggest we continue on with our

journey," the angel said, "and hopefully we'll be able to find medical help for him in Blithe."

"Sounds like a plan," Aaron said after a moment's thought. He reached out and hefted the eighty-pound canine over his shoulder. "Don't worry," he said sarcastically to the angel, grunting with exertion, "I got him."

"Yes, you do," Camael said as he strode into the woods toward the direction of the car.

"Sometimes he bugs the crap out of me," Aaron muttered, following the angel, careful not to stumble with his burden.

"That's just how they are," Gabriel said matter-of-factly.

"How *who* are?"

"Angels."

"What, you're an expert on angels now?"

"Well, I am a complex being," the dog replied haughtily.

chapter four

I am the shaman. They should have listened to me,
Shokad of the Orishas thought as he feverishly
wove his ancient elemental magicks and tun-
neled deep beneath the earth. They never should
have tried to capture the Nephilim—the bones
and stones had told him as much. But did they
listen? No. They let their fear counsel them, the
fear that spoke to their chief during the night,
promising sweet victory. *They should have listened
to me,* he thought bitterly.

His throat as dry as dust from spell casting,
Shokad stopped speaking, and the earth stilled
around him. He leaned close to the curved tunnel wall, looking for signs of life. Careful not to
break it, he pulled a thick, squirming earthworm
from the dirt and popped it into his maw. He
chewed vigorously, the juice from the worm's
muscular body filling his mouth and coating his

throat. He ate his fill, then squatted in the tunnel to rest.

Where do I go from here? the shaman pondered. He closed his eyes, and his mind immediately was filled with blissful images of what could only have been the Safe Place. He saw his people, the ones who had abandoned the Deheboryn many seasons ago, living in harmony with nature, no longer fearing the wrath of the Powers. "They were not killed," he muttered, completely enthralled with the vision. They had managed to evade the wrath of Verchiel and his soldiers, and had found Paradise.

Shokad blessed himself repeatedly, basking in the glory that was the vision of his people thriving within the confines of the Safe Place. It filled him with such joy—and a newfound purpose.

The shaman opened his eyes to the cool darkness of the tunnel and climbed to his feet. He could feel it calling to him now. He could hear it whispering in his ears, drawing him to its secret location. The Safe Place was calling, and all he need do was follow.

He faced the solid wall of dirt before him and recited the ancient words taught by his angelic creators. With these words he could commune with the elements, making them bend to his requests. Shokad asked the dirt wall to allow him passage, and it did as it was asked, flowing around the shaman as he moved toward the promise of Paradise. The wings upon his back flapped eagerly as he trudged through the earth, the Safe Place whispering in his ear, closer—and closer still.

Again he saw them in his mind, those that had left the tribe long ago. *So happy*, he thought. If only Mufgar had had the courage to abandon the old ways, he and Zawar and Tehom could all have experienced the joy that was soon to be his.

The Safe Place was singing now, urging him forward with even greater speed. *You are so close*, it said in a voice filled with promise. *So close to realizing your dream.*

Shokad spoke the words of the spell faster, and the earth in front of him melted away like water. Partly running, partly flying, he burrowed his way toward Paradise, images of those who had come before him in his mind. Suria, Tutrechial, Adririon, Tandal, Savlial: They were all there—some he could have sworn were slain in service to the Powers. It was curious indeed, but he was not about to argue with Paradise.

"Oh, Shokad, you are almost here."

The Orisha began to giggle and angled his tunnel toward the surface. The earth grew thick with rock, making it harder to push forward—but it did not stop him.

"So close, Shokad. So very, very close."

The shaman broke through to the surface. His hands were cracked and bleeding, and the air upon them was cold and damp. *Where is the warm sunshine?* he at first wondered.

Shokad squirmed from the hole in the ground and peered through the eerie greenish light. He found himself in a vast, underground cavern. Somewhere in the distance, beyond the walls of rock, he could hear the rush of water.

"I am here," he said aloud, expecting his people to come forward and welcome him. They did not—but something else moved amongst the rocks at the far end of the cave.

"Greetings," Shokad said as he scrambled toward the noise. It was an odd sound, like something large and heavy being dragged across the rocks. "I am Shokad."

Perhaps they are afraid, he thought as he climbed over the rocky ground, deeper into the cavern. "I mean you no harm," he said aloud. "I, too, have come seeking Paradise."

As he drew closer, he could just barely discern objects in the shadows—fleshy, egglike sacks that hung upon a large, muscular mass, blacker than the cave's deepest shadows. It writhed and pulsed, a thing alive.

"What are you?" Shokad whispered. Cautiously, he stepped forward. "Where are my people?" He stood on tiptoe to peer inside some of the opaque, membranous growths—and his questions were answered.

The Orisha shaman wanted to scream, to ask the divine power that had brought him here why it had shown him this horror, but he didn't have a chance. Something slithered with lightning speed from the shadows behind him and grasped him in its heavy, wet embrace.

Yes, Shokad wanted to scream—for neither he nor his people had found Paradise.

So this is Blithe, Aaron thought as he drove into the center of town. He expected more, but it was much like every other small town they'd driven through in the last two weeks. Quaint old shops, their windows displaying dusty souvenirs, surrounded a grassy common with a fancy white bandstand in its center. It was a beautiful, sunny afternoon, and people strolled in and out of the shops while children played ball in the common.

"How you doing, Gabe?" Aaron asked the dog lying quietly in the backseat.

"I'm okay," Gabriel answered, but Aaron could tell that the dog wasn't feeling all that great.

The Orisha's bite was bad, and it already looked infected. They needed to find a veterinarian soon.

"Hang in there, pal," Aaron said, drawing closer to the town's center. "See any sign of a veterinarian's office?" he asked the angel sitting in the passenger seat beside him.

Camael remained silent, staring out the window with furious intensity, as he had the entire ride to Blithe.

"Hello?" Aaron asked. "What's the story? You see something?"

The angel glanced at him, scowling. "It's nothing," he said, but Aaron knew that something was ruffling his feathers—*pardon the pun.*

"Well, I'm going to ask one of the locals, then," Aaron said as he pulled over in front of a small hardware store.

An older man wearing a soiled Red Sox cap, plaid shirt, and overalls came out of the store with a paper bag and stopped to put his change inside a rubber coin purse.

Aaron reached across Camael, rolled down the passenger window, and called out, "Excuse me!"

The man, his face deeply tanned and criss-crossed with the mileage of age, slipped the change purse into the back pocket of his overalls and stooped slightly to look through the window. His eyes quickly passed suspiciously over everyone in the car.

"Hi," Aaron said in his most friendly voice. He even waved. "I'm hoping you can help us."

The man said nothing, continuing to watch him stoically. Aaron had heard that people in Maine were cautious of strangers, but this was really taking things a bit too far.

Camael meanwhile remained perfectly still, and Aaron wondered if he was willing himself invisible again. Aaron had discovered that he did this from time to time, when he didn't feel like dealing with humans. The last time was two days ago, when they had stopped to walk the dog and were accosted by four elderly sisters who wanted to know everything about Gabriel and Labrador retrievers. Afterward, Aaron told Camael that he was being rude, and the angel responded by saying that it was only because Aaron couldn't yet do it himself.

"My dog was bitten by something in the woods, and I need to get him to a vet."

The old man looked at the dog, his gaze zeroing in on the bite. "What got 'im?" he asked in a raspy voice with a distinctly Maine accent.

"Raccoon," Aaron said quickly. "Sure hope it wasn't rabid."

"Don't look like any 'coon bite I ever seen," the old-timer growled, studying the wound through the open window. "Too wide."

"Well, I only saw it from the back as it ran away. I guess it could have been something else."

The old man glared at Aaron, adjusting the rim of his Red Sox cap. "It wasn't a raccoon—so I guess it *had* to be somethin' else."

Aaron smiled tightly, feeling his patience begin to slip. "Yeah, I guess you're right." He paused and counted to ten. "So I was wondering if there's a vet around here?"

The man seemed to think about it for a minute or two, then slowly nodded his head. "Yep, there is." He fell silent, continuing to stare.

Feeling his blood begin to boil, Aaron wondered how long it would be before Camael summoned a sword and dispatched the annoying old man. "Do you think you could give me directions?" he asked, the strained smile on his face beginning to ache.

Again, the old man thought for a minute, nodded his head slowly, and gave them complex directions to an office just a few miles away.

"That was a rather odd fellow," Camael said as Aaron pulled away from the curb, reviewing the convoluted directions in his mind.

"First meeting with a Mainiac?" Aaron asked, taking a left onto Portland Street, just before a large white church. *"You go beyond that and you've gone too far,"* the old man had stressed.

"I've encountered many madmen in my long years on this planet."

"No, not maniac—*Mainiac*," Aaron explained as he slowly drove down Portland. "People from Maine, that's what they're called."

"Whatever the case, he certainly was odd."

"And you didn't even have to talk to him," Aaron said, on the lookout for a dirt road on the right. "Did you will yourself invisible again?"

"I have no idea what you're talking about," the angel replied, refusing to look at him.

"I'm sure you don't," Aaron said with sarcasm, taking the turn onto a rutted stretch of winding road.

After half a mile, the dirt road opened up into a large, unpaved parking lot. A building to the left of the lot looked as if it had once been a country store with an apartment above. The apartment seemed to still serve that function, but the store-front had been converted into a veterinarian's office. Two sports utility vehicles were parked in the lot, one with Maine plates, the other from Illinois.

"This is it," Aaron said. He parked as close to the building as he could. "Let's get you fixed up, Gabriel."

The dog lifted his head and looked around, his nose twitched and dribbled moisture as he scented the air. *"Where are we?"* he asked.

"The vet," Aaron answered as he got out of the car and opened the back passenger door.

"No we're not," Gabriel said, continuing to sniff at the air. *"We're not in Lynn."*

"This is another office," Aaron explained, leaning into the backseat to check out the wound.

"There's more than one?" Gabriel asked incredulously.

"Lots more than one," Aaron answered as he helped his friend to the ground.

"I never knew that," the dog muttered. He leaned against Aaron for support, holding up his injured leg.

Aaron looked over the top of the car at Camael, who had gotten out and was also sniffing the air. "Are you coming with me?" he asked, squatting down and lifting up the dog.

"No," the angel said succinctly, and turned back toward the dirt road.

"Well, I'm going to be in here for a while if

you need me," Aaron said to the angel's back. Camael continued on without responding. "All right then, Aaron," he muttered to himself as he carefully made his way up the four steps to the front door. A metal placard announced KEVIN WESSELL, DVM. "You take care of Gabriel, and I'll be out here looking around."

Aaron struggled to shift his burden so he could grab the doorknob and turn it. "Thanks for the help, Camael," he said with mock cheeriness. "You certainly are one considerate angelic being."

"Camael's gone," Gabriel reported.

"I know he's gone," Aaron grunted. He turned the knob and pushed the door open with his foot.

"Then why are you still talking to him?"

"I don't know, Gabe," Aaron grumbled as he maneuvered into the small lobby. "These days I do a lot of crazy things."

The place was old, not like the state-of-the art clinic where he had worked in Lynn. The room was done in dark wood paneling, with framed pictures of hunting dogs hung sporadically on the walls. A few plastic seats placed against the wall and an old coffee table covered with magazines and children's books served as the waiting area. The reception desk was straight ahead.

The lobby was deserted, but Aaron could hear the sounds of paper shuffling and a sigh of exasperation coming from behind the desk. He approached and saw a girl surrounded by stacks of paper and medical folders. Her hair was an unusually dark shade of red, and she wore it pulled back in a tight ponytail. Obviously she hadn't heard his entrance, so he cleared his throat and watched as she jumped, startled by his sudden appearance.

"You scared me," she said with a nervous laugh. She moved a stray red hair from her forehead.

"Sorry," Aaron said with a grunt, trying to shift Gabriel's weight in his arms. "Do you think we could see the vet?" he asked.

"Sure," she answered, moving one stack of folders to an even larger one that teetered dangerously. "Just give me a second here and we'll see what we can do."

"I'm . . . I'm not feeling so good, Aaron," Gabriel whined in his arms.

The dog shivered and Aaron guessed that a fever was brewing. He felt his temper spike. He'd already wasted enough time with the Mainiac in the Red Sox cap; he wasn't about to let his dog suffer anymore. "Look," he said rather forcefully, "I'll fill out all the forms you have, but could you please get the doctor out here? I think he's got a pretty nasty infection, and I want to get some antibiotics into him as soon as possible. . . ."

"All right, all right," the redhead said as she stood and moved around the counter. "Let's take him in back and I'll give him a look." She motioned for them to follow.

"You're not Dr. Wessell," Aaron said, taken aback.

"No," she responded. "But I almost was. I'm just plain Katie McGovern right now." She laughed. "But not to worry, I'm also a licensed veterinarian."

Aaron laughed self-consciously as he carried Gabriel toward the examination room. "I'm sorry, I didn't mean to come off like a jerk, it's just that it's been a really long day and I thought you were—"

"The receptionist?" she asked. She opened the door to the exam room and stepped back for him to enter.

"Yeah," he answered. "You don't look old enough to—"

"I'm twenty-seven," she said, closing the door. "The product of fine Irish genes. I can show you my diploma from the University of Illinois College of Veterinary Medicine," she added as she helped him lay Gabriel on the metal table. "How you doing, buddy?" she asked the dog, stroking his head and rubbing his ears.

"My name's not Buddy," Gabriel growled. *"It's Gabriel."*

"His name is Gabriel," Aaron told her.

"Hello there, Gabriel," Katie said as she slipped on a pair of rubber gloves. "Let's take a look and see what we can do about fixing you up." She examined the wound in his leg, gently prodding the seeping injury. "What did you say bit him?" she asked.

"I think it was a raccoon," Aaron answered lamely.

"A raccoon?" she questioned, looking up from the oozing bite. "If that's a raccoon bite, I'm a teenage receptionist."

Camael could feel it on the breeze—one of many strange things he could sense ever since he finally arrived in the town of Blithe.

He walked slowly down Portland Street, taking a right as he left the stretch of dirt road. Something in the atmosphere told him that he belonged here, that he was welcome—but there was also something else, something he couldn't identify. It was an odd sensation hidden beneath layers of other, far more pleasant impulses.

The angel widened his perceptions as he turned onto Acadia Street. It was as quiet as death here, void of life, the only sounds the gentle hiss of the warm presummer breeze and the pounding of the surf far off in the distance. Offices lined both sides of the short street: Johnson's Realtors, McNulty Certified Public Accountants, Dr. Charles Speegal, Optometrist, and the largest building belonging to the Carroll Funeral Home, which took up almost one whole side of the street.

Everything about this town said that he was

supposed to be here. It disarmed him, made him think about and feel things he had not experienced in thousands of years. There was an unwarranted contentment here, and the angel wondered if he and Aaron had indeed stumbled across the haven that was Aerie. He crossed the street to stand before the white, two-story building that was the Carroll Funeral Home, and looked around carefully. *But then, where are the others?*

Again came that wave of sensation he could not immediately identify, like a great beast of the sea breaking the surface for air before diving again beneath the dark, murky depths. But this time there was something in it that he finally recognized: the scent of an ethereal presence trying very hard to hide beneath sensations of serenity. Now that he had the scent, he had to be careful not to lose it. It was old, very, very old—a whiff of chaos that had not been breathed since the days of creation.

Camael heard the sound of a door opening and turned back to face the funeral home, willing himself invisible. An old man, dressed in a dark suit and tie, was standing on the top step, looking down at him. Camael was perplexed; it was as if he were able to see the angel—but of course, that was impossible.

The feelings of tranquility tripled, bombarding Camael with sensations meant to keep him complacent, but he held on to the ancient scent. No matter how hard it tried to hide beneath the oceans of serenity radiating from the town, he knew that at the core of Blithe there was chaos.

The man continued to stare at him with eyes black and deep, and Camael knew that the man in the suit could see him. "How is this possible?" Camael asked.

The old man's head cocked to one side strangely, and he smiled. Then he blinked slowly, and Camael noticed a milky, membranous covering over his eyes. Not something that he had ever perceived on the human anatomy before. Sensing that he might be in danger, Camael was about to summon a weapon of fire when the old man leaned forward, his bones creaking painfully, and coughed. Tiny projectiles, about the size of a cherry, and barbed, were expelled from his mouth to stick in Camael's face and neck.

The angel scowled angrily, reaching up to pluck the offensive matter from his flesh when he felt his body growing numb. "Poison," he grumbled, tearing one of the barbed projectiles from his face and staring at it. It was brown and pulsed with an organic life of its own. It was the second time that day that some primitive form of life had attempted to vanquish him using toxins.

Camael closed his eyes and willed the poison from his body. Shockingly, it did little good, and he found that he did not have the strength to open his eyes again. The world seemed to tilt beneath his feet, and he fell to the ground.

Through the darkness behind his eyes, he heard the sound of the old man's feet as he shuffled down the stairs toward him. Pulled deeper and deeper into the clutches of unconsciousness, Camael was consoled by the town of Blithe.

"You were meant to be here," it said, easing the angel on his way into oblivion. *"For without you, I would die."*

Aaron petted Gabriel as he watched Dr. McGovern shave away the fur on the dog's leg, then squirt some saline solution into the wound. She dabbed at it with a cotton swab and leaned in to examine it more closely.

"Mouths are filthy, so I just assume that all bites are infected," she said, squirting more saline into the wound. "This one is particularly nasty, though—especially for a raccoon bite." She looked up to catch Aaron's eye.

"I said I thought it was a raccoon," he responded, flustered. No way was he going to explain that Gabriel had been bitten by a nasty little creature created by fallen angels. "I didn't get that good of a look at it—I guess it could have been just about anything."

"It was an Orisha, Aaron," Gabriel grumbled.

"I know, I know," Aaron said reassuringly.

"He's pretty vocal, isn't he?" The vet threw the soiled cotton swabs into a barrel, then rubbed Gabriel's head affectionately.

"You don't know the half of it," Aaron replied with a sly smile and a chuckle. "Say, is he going to need a rabies booster?"

"*A shot?*" Gabriel grunted, lifting his head from the table.

"When did he get his last vaccination?" Dr. McGovern asked.

"*I just got a shot,*" the Lab whined.

"About six months ago," Aaron said, ignoring his best friend.

"Yeah, why don't we do a booster, then. Better to be safe than sorry," she said, pulling a syringe from a drawer and getting a vial of vaccine from a tiny fridge beneath the counter.

"*Better no shot than sorry,*" Gabriel growled.

"He doesn't sound too happy," the vet said, filling the needle.

"He's not, but he doesn't have a choice. He has to get a shot or else *he'll get sick.*" Aaron emphasized the last of the sentence specifically to the dog.

"Do you think he understands you?"

"I know he does," Aaron answered, rubbing the thick fur around Gabriel's neck. "This guy is pretty special."

"Aren't they all," she said, and with one quick move, administered the injection with not so much as a yelp from the dog. "See," she cooed, leaning into Gabriel's face and rubbing his ears. "That wasn't so bad, was it?"

"*She smells good, Aaron,*" the dog woofed, his

large, muscular tail thumping happily on the metal table.

Aaron laughed. "Don't worry, Gabriel doesn't hold many grudges. Give 'im some affection and a cookie and he'll forget all about the trauma."

The doctor disposed of the syringe in a red plastic container on the counter. "All right," she said, looking over her notes. "Let's see, keep the wound uncovered so it can dry out and . . ."

"Warm compresses three times a day and two weeks of amoxicillin twice daily to kill the infection," Aaron continued as he watched Gabriel sit up carefully on the table.

Dr. McGovern smiled, setting her pen down. "Pretty good." She nodded. "Do we have an interest in the veterinary sciences?"

"I used to work in a vet's office," Aaron explained, the recollection of the life he had left behind washing over him in a wave of melancholy. He quickly turned back to Gabriel. "Do you want to get down?"

"Let me help you," the vet said, and together they lowered Gabriel to the floor.

"You know," she said, "I'm only here temporarily—but I could use a hand around the office. I can't pay great money, but I could pay you something, and I could look after Gabriel's bite—what do you say?"

It certainly was a tempting offer. There was something about this little town that had really gotten into Aaron's system. It seemed to be saying that *this* was the place where he wanted to be. The fact that he could earn some money to bolster his dwindling savings account wasn't a bad idea either. "Shouldn't you check with Dr. Wessell first?" he asked.

Dr. McGovern nodded slowly. "I imagine so, but since my former fiancé is nowhere to be found, I'd say that gives me leeway to bend the rules a bit. You interested?"

"Let's stay, Aaron," Gabriel whined. *"I'm tired of the car."*

"I'd have to check with my traveling companion," Aaron said with a shrug. "But sure, if it's okay with him, I'd love to hang around for a couple days."

"Great," she said, extending her hand. "I'm Katie, and I know this is Gabriel, but it might be nice to know your name, too, especially if we'll be working together."

"Sorry." He took her hand in his and gave it a shake. "Aaron," he said. "Aaron Corbet."

"Great to meet you, Aaron." She released his hand. "Why don't you go check with your friend and let me know what you'll be doing."

Aaron and Gabriel stepped from the building into the warm, spring afternoon and headed for the car. Gabriel was able to walk on his own with a minimum of discomfort, thanks to Katie's ministrations.

"Where's Camael?" Gabriel asked as Aaron

opened the door and helped him into the back-seat. He immediately lay down to check out the wound on his leg, sniffing and licking at the antiseptic goo that covered it.

"I don't know," Aaron answered. "And leave your leg alone," he added, looking around for signs of the angel.

Since the battle at his home, he and the former Powers' commander had formed a strange kind of bond. Aaron was always aware of the angel's presence, and although he could feel something unusual about Blithe, right now he felt no sense at all of Camael. That alone was troubling. *Looks like we* will *be staying a while*, he thought.

At that moment, Katie came outside to get supplies from the back of her truck.

"Stay here a minute," Aaron told Gabriel, jogging over to the vet, who was trying to balance three large boxes in her arms and close the back of her SUV.

"Katie, looks like I'll be taking you up on your offer," he said as she peeked out from behind the teetering boxes.

"Great," she replied. "And your first assignment?"

Aaron snapped to attention. "Sure, what's that?"

"Give your boss a hand with these boxes," she said. "Damn things are heavy."

chapter five

"**W**here do you think he went?" Gabriel asked from the backseat as Aaron continued his patrol of Blithe.

"I have no idea," he said, scanning the streets for signs of the wayward Camael. "Maybe he found another Nephilim he likes better and skipped town."

"*Do you think he would do that?*" Gabriel asked, aghast.

"I'm just kidding." Aaron chuckled as he eyed a coffee shop.

An elderly couple came out of the shop, and Aaron tried to see inside as the door slowly closed—but no luck. *Besides, why would he be in a coffee shop—he doesn't even have to eat*, Aaron thought as he brought his car to a stop at a crosswalk, allowing an older woman with a shopping cart to cross. *But then again, they might have had French fries.*

In the rearview mirror he watched the Labrador tilt his head back and sniff the air. *"Do you want me to get out and see if I can find him?"* Gabriel asked. *"I might be able to pick up his scent. He does smell kind of funny, you know."*

"No, that's all right, Gabe," Aaron replied. "He'll turn up. Why don't we just find some-place to stay that'll take pets."

"I'm much more than a pet," the dog said with pride.

"So you've told me," Aaron responded, tak-ing a left onto Berkely Street. "Katie said there's a place that rents rooms down here."

At the end of the dead-end street stood a large, white house surrounded by a jungle of colorful wildflowers. A wooden ROOMS FOR RENT sign moved in the breeze.

"There it is," he said, pulling to the curb in front of the house and turning off the engine. "You stay here. I'll go find out how much they charge and if they allow pets."

"You tell them I am not just a pet, Gabriel called through the open window as Aaron headed up the walk beneath a wooden arch bedecked with snaking purple flowers.

"Can I help you?" asked an aged voice from somewhere amongst the lush vegetation.

"Yeah," he responded, startled, not sure where to direct his answer. "I'm looking for a room."

An old woman emerged from behind a thick forsythia bush, sharp-looking pruning sheers in her hand. She glared at him through thick, dark-framed sunglasses that made her look like one of the X-Men, and wiped some sweat from her brow with a glove-covered hand. "I have a few—ain't that a coincidence."

Aaron laughed nervously. "Cool," he said with what he hoped was a charming smile.

"You alone, or with somebody?" She craned her neck to get a look at the car parked on the street. "Thought I heard you talkin' to somebody."

"I was talking to my dog," he said, studying her face for a response.

The woman scowled. "You got a dog?"

Aaron nodded slowly.

"You want me to rent you a room—with a dog?" she asked incredulously.

He sighed. "Sorry to have wasted your time," he said with a polite wave as he hastily turned and headed back toward the car.

He was just beneath the flowered archway when he heard the woman's voice very close behind him. "What kind of dog is it?"

"He's a yellow labrador," Aaron answered, not quite sure what difference it made.

"Yellow?" she repeated, eyeing his vehicle.

Aaron nodded. "Yellow Lab, yes."

She followed him as he continued to the car. "My father used to raise Labs," she said as she pulled off her work gloves and stuck them in the back pockets of her worn blue jeans. "Sometimes I have a soft spot for them."

Aaron opened the back door of the car, exposing Gabriel. "Hey Gabe," he said, "somebody wants to meet you."

The old woman kept her distance, but crouched to peer into the car. Gabriel panted happily and wagged his tail against the back of the seat. It sounded like a drumbeat.

"What did you call him?" she asked, removing her funky shades, giving him a lesser version of the scowl from the yard.

"Gabriel."

"That's a good name." She stared into the car. "What happened to his leg?" she asked, pointing at the nasty wound.

"Oh, he got bit by a—a possum, I think," Aaron said. "That's one of the reasons why we're looking for a place to stay. The leg needs to heal a bit before we move on."

"That ain't no possum bite," the old woman said with a shake of her head. She leaned into the car and let Gabriel sniff her bony, callused hands. "What bit you, boy?" she asked, petting his head.

"I think it was called an Orisha," Gabriel woofed.

"Would you look at that," she said with a genuine smile. "You'd think he was trying to answer me."

"He's very talkative," Aaron said, giving Gabriel a thumbs-up behind the woman's back.

"He housebroke?" she asked, still rubbing

the dog's velvety soft ears and stroking the side of his face.

"Of course he is," Aaron answered, holding his indignation in check. "And he doesn't bark or chew. Gabriel's just an all-around good dog."

She emerged from the car and gave Aaron the once-over. "Well, you don't look like a Rockefeller, so it'll be a hundred dollars a week, with meals—but you have to eat with me. This ain't no restaurant."

"That's great," he answered cheerily. "It'll be nice to have something other than fast food for a change."

The old woman studied him for a minute, then turned and began to walk up the path into her yard. "Don't go thanking me yet," she said, placing her sunglasses back on her face and removing the work gloves from her pockets. "Never told you if I was a good cook or not."

She stopped suddenly and turned back to him. "Since you're gonna be living underneath my roof for a bit, you might as well tell me your name."

"It's Aaron," he said with a smile. "Aaron Corbet."

"Aaron," she said a few times, committing it to memory. "I'm Mrs. Provost—used to be Orville, but after my husband died in seventy-two, I figured I'd go back to my maiden name. Never cared for much he gave me, especially the name."

She continued on her way up the path, tugging the gloves on her hands as she walked.

"Well, are you?" he suddenly asked her.

She stopped and turned around with that nasty scowl decorating her face. "Am I what?" she asked, annoyed.

"Are you a good cook?" he asked with a grin.

Try as she might to hold it back, Mrs. Provost cracked a smile, but quickly turned around so Aaron could not see it for long. "Depends on who you ask," she said, picking up the pruning sheers from the steps leading to the front porch. "My husband thought I was pretty good—but look how he ended up."

"It's nice," Aaron said as he walked into the room and looked around.

The theme was grapes. There were grape lamp shades, a vase with grapevines painted on its side; even the bedspread had grapes on it. It was kind of funky, but he thought it was cool. Gabriel hobbled in and immediately found a place to lie down beside the queen-size bed where the warm sunlight streamed through the window.

"Is that where he'll sleep?" Mrs. Provost asked.

The floor is good, but sometimes I like to sleep with Aaron, Gabriel barked.

"Is that where you'd like him to sleep?" Aaron asked with a sly smile.

"He can sleep wherever the hell he wants,"

she said, moving toward the closet. She opened the door and pulled out a white comforter adorned with grapes. "Just thought if he was going to sleep on the floor, he might be more comfortable lying on this."

As she approached, Gabriel got up and let her place the downy bedspread in the patch of sunlight. "There you go, boy," she said, smoothing out the material. "Give this a try."

And the dog did just that, lying back on the comforter with a heavy sigh of exhaustion.

"I think your dog's tired," she said, reaching into her blue jeans pocket. She handed Aaron a key on an I-LOVE-MAINE chain. "Here's your key. It works on the front door, too, which I lock promptly at nine o'clock every night." Mrs. Provost moved toward the door. "I eat supper at six," she said as she walked out into the hall. "If you like meat loaf, I'll see you in the kitchen. If not, you're on your own."

"I like meat loaf," Gabriel yipped from his bed as the old woman closed the door behind her.

"Is there any food you *don't* like?" Aaron asked, kneeling down to check the injured leg.

"Never really thought about it," Gabriel replied thoughtfully.

"Tell you what," Aaron said, patting his head. "Why don't you give that question some serious thought while I go see if I can find Camael."

"Will you be all right?"

"I'll be fine." Aaron climbed to his feet and walked to the door. He was just about to leave when Gabriel called.

"Aaron, do you think we'll find Stevie here?"

Aaron thought for a moment, trying to make sense of the odd feelings that were still with him. "I don't know. Let me poke around a little and we'll talk later." Then he left, leaving his best friend alone to rest and heal.

Aaron strolled casually up Berkely Street, taking in his surroundings. He turned left onto a street with no sign, committing landmarks to memory so he wouldn't get lost. Lots of quaint homes, nicely kept up, many with beautiful flower gardens more tame than Mrs. Provost's version of the Amazon rain forest.

At the end of the nameless street he stopped to assess his whereabouts. There was still no sign of Camael, and the bizarre sensation he'd been feeling since arriving in Blithe continued to trouble him. It felt as though he'd had too much caffeine after a late night of studying. He knew he had the ability to interpret this strange feeling, but he didn't know how to go about it. There was still so much he had to learn about this whole Nephilim thing.

"You will need to master these abilities," Camael had said during their ride to Blithe. *"Sooner rather than later."*

Aaron found the angel's words somewhat

annoying. Mastering these so-called abilities was like reading a book without knowing the alphabet. He just didn't have the basics.

He recalled a moment not long after they'd first left Lynn. Camael had been describing how an angel experiences the five senses—not as individual sensations, but as one overpowering perception of everything around it. *"Do as I do,"* the angel had said to him, closing his eyes. *"Feel the world and everything that makes it a whole, as only beings of our stature can."* Aaron had tried, but only ended up with a nasty headache. Camael had clearly been disappointed—apparently Aaron just wasn't turning out to be the Nephilim that the former leader of the Powers thought he should be. *Maybe it's not me the seer wrote about in the prophecy,* he thought. *Maybe Camael's finally realized this, and took off to find the fallen angels' real savior.*

Something rustled in a patch of woods behind him, and Aaron turned toward the noise. He noticed a glint of red in a patch of shadow, and then, as if knowing that it had been discovered, a raccoon slowly emerged from its hiding place. *This is odd,* Aaron thought, watching the animal. *I thought raccoons are nocturnal.* He recalled how he'd hear them late at night through his bedroom window as they tried to get into the sealed trash barrels.

The raccoon moved closer, its large dark eyes unwavering. It was moving strangely, and he wondered if it was rabid. *"Is that it?"* he asked aloud, knowing instinctively that the animal would understand him. *"Are you rabid?"*

The raccoon did not respond. It just continued to stare, and pad steadily closer.

As Aaron gazed into its eyes, an overwhelming sense of euphoria washed over him. It was all he could do to keep from bursting out in laughter and then breaking down in tears of sheer joy. He closed his eyes and swayed with the waves of emotion.

Stevie. His little brother was *here*—in Blithe, he was sure of it. Aaron could feel him, waiting to be picked up—embraced, played with. Stevie was unharmed, and that brought Aaron the greatest pleasure he had ever felt. Nothing would ever come between them again.

"Excuse me," a voice suddenly interrupted his reverie.

Aaron opened his eyes and saw that the odd raccoon was gone, replaced by a police officer who was eyeing him strangely. "Is there a problem, sir?" the policeman asked him, moving closer, his hand clutching his gun belt.

Aaron swayed, feeling as though he'd been on a roller coaster. "I'm fine," he managed. *What just happened?*

"You don't seem fine," the officer barked. "You been drinking?" he asked, stepping closer to sniff Aaron's breath.

Aaron shook his head, feeling his strength

and wits slowly returning. "No sir, I'm fine. I think I might have sunstroke or something."

"Can I ask you what you're doing here?"

"Actually, I'm looking for a friend of mine," Aaron said, bringing a hand up to his brow to wipe away beads of sweat. "Tall, silvery white hair and goatee, dressed in a dark suit?"

The policeman continued to watch him through his mirrored glasses. "I'd like to see some identification," he finally said, holding out his hand.

Aaron was getting nervous. First Camael disappears, then the strange raccoon—and now an evil sheriff. As he handed the police officer his license, he couldn't help but wonder what other surprises the town of Blithe had in store for him.

"Just passing through Blithe, Mr. Corbet?" the policeman asked, handing back his identification.

Aaron returned the license to his wallet. "I'll probably be here for a couple of days," he said, sliding his wallet into his back pocket. Suddenly Aaron couldn't help himself; the attitude he had worked so hard to keep in check was rearing its ugly head. It had been the bane of his existence— he just couldn't learn to keep his mouth shut. "Is there a problem, Officer . . . ?" he asked, an edge to his tone.

"Dexter," the policeman said, touching the rim of his hat. "*Chief of Police* Dexter. And no, there isn't any problem—now." He smiled, but Aaron saw little emotion in it. If anything, it appeared more like a snarl than a smile. "Blithe is a quiet town, Mr. Corbet, and it's my job to make sure it stays that way, if you catch my meaning."

Aaron nodded, biting his tongue. After all, he was a stranger, and evidently that made him immediately suspect.

Chief Dexter began to walk toward a cruiser parked by the side of the road nearby. Aaron had been so caught up in the bizarre spell of raw emotion that he hadn't even heard the policeman pull up. He looked back to the wooded area. "Chief Dexter?" he called.

The policeman stopped, his hand on the door handle of his cruiser.

"You didn't happen to see a raccoon when you pulled up here, did you?" Aaron asked.

Dexter pulled open the door, and the squawk from his radio drifted out to fill the still air of the neighborhood. He smiled that nasty, snarling smile again before easing himself into the driver's seat. "No raccoons around this time of day, Mr. Corbet. They're nocturnal."

"Thought so." Aaron nodded. He stared at the police officer. There was something about him . . .

"Enjoy your visit, Mr. Corbet," Chief Dexter said. "Hope you find your friend," he added, before slamming closed the door of his car, banging a U-turn, and driving away.

† † †

From a woman who brought her dog in for its annual heartworm check, Katie McGovern learned that her former fiancé had been missing for at least four days. Apparently, the dog—an eight-year-old poodle named Taffy—had had an appointment for Monday morning, but no one had been in the office until Katie arrived that Wednesday afternoon. *It's very unlike Dr. Wessell to miss an appointment. I hope everything is all right*, the dog's middle-aged owner had said, her voice touched with concern.

Katie had made up a story about a family emergency that Kevin would have to deal with when he finally got back—*if he does*, said a nasty little voice at the back of her mind. She had tried to ignore the voice by cleaning up the office and catching up with Kevin's appointments. *From organization comes order*, her mother had always said. *And from order comes answers.* But the creeping unease she'd been feeling in the pit of her stomach since receiving that first e-mail from her former lover a little over two weeks ago continued to grow.

Think I've found something here that might interest you—care for a visit? Katie had thought it nothing more than another attempt by Kevin to get her back into his life, and she'd ignored the message—until she received another a few days later.

Not sure if I can handle this. Really need to see you. Please come.

There was a certain urgency in the communication that had piqued her curiosity. She had called him the next day, but there was no answer at the clinic. And when Kevin had failed to return the multiple messages she'd left on his home phone over several days, she'd decided to take some vacation time and head to Maine. They may have broken up nearly two years earlier, but it didn't mean they weren't still friends.

The office had been in complete disarray—Kevin did have a tendency to become easily distracted. In fact it was a *distraction* with another woman that had brought an end to their relationship. But this was different.

Katie glanced at her watch; it was nearly six, and she felt as though she hadn't stopped to breathe all afternoon—between appointments, trying to bring order to the place, and figure out where Kevin had gone. She thought of Aaron Corbet. He seemed just the person to help her keep the practice afloat during Kevin's absence.

She snatched up his dog's file from the corner of the desk and casually began to review it. The words "raccoon bite" stuck out like a sore thumb. Katie had seen many bites in her years as a vet—and Gabriel's hadn't been caused by any raccoon. She wasn't even sure if the bite had come from anything that walked on four legs. In fact, the wound looked as though it might have been made by a small child. *Something else to add to the strangeness of Blithe,* she thought.

The veterinarian sighed and closed the folder.

She moved to the file cabinet next to the desk and pulled open the drawer. Katie added Gabriel's file to the others she had organized and tried to slide it closed. But something was blocking it. She reached in and felt behind the drawer. Sometimes a file slipped out of place and became wedged in the sliding track. Her hand closed on what felt like a book. She tugged it free and slammed the drawer shut.

Probably some veterinary journal, she mused, bringing it to the desk to take a look. It was a journal, all right, but one of a far more personal nature: Kevin's journal. She remembered him writing in it each night before bed. It was something he had started in college. *Helps me get my thoughts in order,* he had told her one night when she'd asked him about the habit.

She flipped through the entries and stopped at the one dated June 1:

> *Saw another one today on my hike. I'd swear they were watching me. Gives me the creeps. Wonder what Katie would think.*

That was right about the time she had received his first e-mail. With a churning sensation in the pit of her stomach, Katie turned to the date closest to the last message he had sent:

> *June 8: Found another one and put it in the freezer with the rest. Don't know what the*

cause is. Don't want to alarm the locals YET. Never in all my years have I seen anything like it. I wonder if it has anything to do with how strangely the local fauna's been acting lately. I still swear they're watching me. I need somebody else to see this—somebody I trust. I'm going to ask Katie to come. I'm feeling a little spooked right now, and it'll be good to see her.

"What the hell are you talking about?" Katie said to the journal, her frustration on the rise. It was the last entry and, like the others, it told her very little.

Katie tossed the journal onto the desktop and thought about what she had read. "You found something and put it in the freezer," she said to herself, chewing at the end of her fingernail. Her eyes scanned the reception area, and she bolted to her feet. "All right, let's take a look, then." She hadn't seen a freezer, although most veterinarians kept large units to store deceased animals, tissue samples, and other specimens. *There must be one around here somewhere*, she thought.

She moved away from the desk and strolled down the hallway past the examination room. At the end of the hall was a door that she had originally thought was to a maintenance closet. Katie grabbed hold of the doorknob, turned it, and found herself looking down a flight of wooden steps that disappeared into the darkness of a cellar.

She felt for a light switch along the wall and, finding none, used the cool stone for a guide as she carefully descended. At the foot of the stairs she could just make out the iridescent shape of a lightbulb that seemed to be suspended in the darkness. She reached out, fumbled for the chain, and gave it a good yank.

The bulb came to life, illuminating the cool storage area dug out from the rock and dirt beneath the building's foundation. She recognized Kevin's mountain bike, ski equipment, and even a canoe, but it was the freezer in the far corner that attracted her interest. Plugged into a heavy-duty socket beneath a gray metal electrical box, the white unit sat atop some wooden pallets, humming quietly.

Maneuvering around winter coats hanging from pipes, Katie approached the freezer. She stood in front of the oblong unit, feeling a faint aura of cold radiating from the white box. Her fingers began to tingle in anticipation as she slowly reached for the cover.

"Let's see what spooked you, Kev," she said in a whisper, lifting up the lid. A cloud of freezing air billowed up, and she breathed the cold gas into her lungs, coughing. The distinctive aroma of frozen dead things filled the air, and she took note of the red biohazard symbols on the bags lying along the freezer bottom. She leaned into the chest, reaching down to pick up one of the bags. It was covered in a fine frost, masking its contents, and Katie brushed away the icy coating so she could see within the thick biohazard container. The thing inside the bag stared back with eyes frozen wide in death.

"Holy crap," Katie McGovern said as she studied the specimen through the plastic bag. A creeping unease ran up and down the length of her spine, making her shudder. "No wonder you were freaked out."

interlude two

Stevie Stanley huddled in a dark corner of his mind, trying with all his might to hold on to the things that made him who he was—those pockets of recollection, moments that had left their indelible marks on his fragile psyche. But the excruciating pain was systematically ripping those memories away. One after another they disappeared: the blue, blue sky filled with birds; the black-and-gray static on the television screen; the yellow dog running in the yard with a red ball in his mouth; Mom and Dad holding him, kissing him. And Aaron—his protector, his playmate—so beautiful.

So beautiful.

Seven Archons surrounded the child's writhing body and continued the ritual that so often ended with the death of the subject. Stevie fought wildly against his restraints as Archon Jaldabaoth painted the symbols of transfiguration upon his pale, naked skin, muttering sounds and words that a human mouth could never manage. Archon Oraios stabbed a long, gold needle into the child's stomach and depressed the plunger to implant the magickal seeds of change.

The sigils on Stevie's flesh then began to rise, to smolder—to burn. The boy screamed wildly as his body was racked with the painful changes. Archon Jao placed a delicate hand over the child's mouth to silence his irksome cries. Things were proceeding nicely, and the Archons waited patiently as the transformation progressed.

Soon there would be nothing left of Stevie. His memory of Aaron burned the brightest, its loving warmth providing some insulation against the agony his tiny, seven-year-old body was forced to endure. Aaron would come for him. Aaron would rescue him from the pain; he need only hold on to what little he still had.

Archon Sabaoth was the first to notice. He tilted his head and listened. Sounds were coming from the child's body—other than the muffled screams of his discomfort. Cracking, grinding, ripping, and tearing sounds: the boy's body had begun to change—to grow—to mature beyond his seven years. This was the most dangerous part of the ritual, and the Archons studied their subject with unblinking eyes, searching for signs that the magicks might have gone awry.

Archon Katspiel remembered a subject whose

bone structure had grown disproportionately, leaving the poor creature hideously deformed. Its mind had been so psychologically damaged by the pain that they'd had no choice but to order Archon Domiel to put it out of its misery. It had been a shame, really, for that subject had shown great potential—almost as much as this latest effort.

Stevie held on as long as he could, clutching at the final memory of his brother, friend, and protector—but it was slipping away, piece by jagged piece. He wanted to hold on to it, to remember the beautiful face of the boy who had promised never to leave him, but the pain—there was so much of it. *What was the boy's name?* he wondered as he curled up within himself, no longer knowing the question, no longer caring. It didn't matter. Now there was only pain. He was the pain—and the pain was he.

Archon Erathaol unlocked the manacles around the subject's chafed wrists and ankles while the others watched. *The ritual appears to have been successful*, he mused as they watched the subject curl into a fetal position on the floor of the solarium. What had once been a frail child was now a mature adult, his body altered to physical perfection, and his sensitivity to the preternatural greatly augmented. The Archons had succeeded in their task.

Verchiel would be pleased.

chapter six

It was quite possibly the best meat loaf Aaron had ever had. He shoveled the last bit of mashed potatoes and peas into his mouth, leaving a good bite of meat loaf uneaten. Gabriel lay beside his chair looking up pathetically, a puddle of drool between his paws.

Aaron looked at Mrs. Provost across the kitchen table. She was sipping a cup of instant coffee—*made with the coffee bags, not that granule crap*, she had informed him.

"Do you mind?" he asked, pointing at the piece of meat covered in dark brown gravy and motioning toward the dog.

"I don't care," she said, taking a sip of her coffee. "Would have given him his own plate if you'd'a let me."

Aaron picked up the meat and gave it to Gabriel. "He had his supper, and besides, too much people-food isn't good for him," he said as the dog greedily gobbled the meat from his fingers, making certain to lick every ounce of grease and gravy from the digits. "Makes him gassy."

"Are you trying to embarrass me?" Gabriel grunted, licking his chops.

Aaron laughed and ruffled the yellow dog's velvety soft ears.

"That's something I can relate to," the old woman said, hauling herself up from her seat. "Some days I feel like that blimp for the tires, I'm so full a' gas."

Aaron stifled a laugh.

She reached across the table for his plate and stacked it atop hers. "Meal couldn't a' been too bad," she said, staring at his empty plate. "I don't even have to wash this one," she said with a wise smirk.

"Didn't mean to be a pig," Aaron said as Mrs. Provost took the dirty dishes to the sink. "It was really good. Thanks again."

She turned on the water and started washing the dishes. Aaron thought about asking if he could do that for her, but something told him she would probably just say something nasty, so he kept his offer to himself. When she wanted him to do something, he was certain she wouldn't be shy in asking.

"I was cooking for myself, anyway," Mrs. Provost said, wiping one of the dinner plates with a sponge shaped like an apple. "And besides, it's kinda nice to have company to supper every once in a while."

Aaron wondered if the old woman was lonely since the death of her husband. He hadn't seen any evidence of children or grandchildren.

"Then again, cooking for somebody else can be a real pain in the ass after a while . . . makes you remember why you was eatin' by yourself in the first place."

Well, maybe she was just fine after all. . . .

She left the dishes in the strainer and hung the damp towel over the metal rack attached to the front of the cabinet below the sink. Then she returned to the table to finish her coffee. Aaron wasn't sure if he should thank her and go to his room, or stay and chat. The kitchen was quiet except for the hum of the refrigerator in the corner and Gabriel's rhythmic breathing as he drifted off to sleep.

"Where you from, Aaron?" Mrs. Provost abruptly asked as she brought her coffee mug to her mouth.

"I'm from Lynn—Lynn, Massachusetts," he clarified.

"Didn't think it was Lynn, North Dakota," the old woman replied, setting her mug down on the gray speckled tabletop. "The city of sin, huh? Family there?"

His expression must have changed dramatically, because he saw a look of uncertainty in her eyes. He didn't want her to feel bad, so he responded the best way he knew how. "I did," he said as he looked at his hands lying flat on the table. "They died in a fire a few weeks back."

"I'm sorry," Mrs. Provost said, gripping her coffee cup in both hands.

Aaron smiled at her. "It's all right," he said. "Really. It's why I'm in Maine right now. You know, change of scenery to try to clear my head."

She nodded. "Thought about leaving here once myself—about the time I met my husband," she said, a faraway look in her eye. "Never did, though. Ended up getting married instead."

Mrs. Provost abruptly stood and brought her coffee mug to the sink. Gabriel awoke with a start and lifted his head from the floor, wanting to be sure he wasn't missing anything. Aaron reached down and stroked the top of his head. "So you never left Blithe?" he asked her as she rinsed the cup.

"Nope." She put the cup in the drainer with the other dishes. "But I often think about what might've happened if I had—if my life woulda been different."

It was becoming uncomfortable in the kitchen, and Aaron found himself blurting out a question before he could think about it. "Do you have any children?"

Mrs. Provost wiped her hands on the dish-towel and began to straighten up her countertop. "I have a son—Jack. He lives with his wife and daughter in San Diego." She had retrieved the apple sponge from the sink and was wiping down the tops of her canister set. "We were never that close, my son and I," she said. "After Luke died—that was my husband—we just grew further and further apart."

"Have you ever gone to visit them?" Aaron asked, suspecting he already knew the answer.

"Nope," she said, wiping the countertop for a second time. "They bought me one of those computers last year for Christmas so we could keep in touch with e-mail and all, but I think that Internet is up to something. That and the Home Shopping Network."

"You have a computer?" Aaron was suddenly excited. It had been days since he'd last had an opportunity to check his e-mail and communicate with Vilma.

"It's what I said, isn't it?" Mrs. Provost pointed toward the parlor. "It's in the office off the parlor," she said. "My son insists on paying for it even though I never touch the thing. You can use it if you want."

"Thanks," he said.

"But don't go looking up no porno," she warned, placing the apple sponge back where it belonged beside the sink. "I don't tolerate no porno in this house—that and the Home Shopping Network."

† † †

Camael knew that he wasn't in Aerie, but a voice in his mind tried to convince him it was so.

"Calm yourself, angel," said the hissing presence nestled within his fervid thoughts. *"This is what you have sought."*

He wanted so much to believe it, to succumb to the wishes of the comforting tongue and finally let down his defenses.

"Welcome to Aerie, Camael," it cooed. *"We've been waiting so long for you to arrive."*

An image of Aaron—the Nephilim—flickered in his mind. *If this is indeed Aerie, he'll need to be brought here,* Camael thought as he attempted to move within the thick, viscous fluid surrounding him. Muscular tendrils tightened around his body, holding him firm.

"There is no need for concern," the voice spoke soothingly. *"The boy will come in time. This is* your *moment, warrior. Let yourself go, and allow Aerie to be everything you have desired."*

The membranous sack around him began to thrum, a rhythmic pulsing meant to lull him deeper into complacency. The heartbeat of asylum.

"Let your guard down, angel," the voice ordered. *"You cannot possibly experience all you have yearned for—until you give yourself completely to me."*

Deep down, Camael knew this was wrong. He wanted to fight it, to summon a sword of fire and burn away the insensate cloud that seemed to envelop his mind—but he just didn't have the strength.

"Your doubts are an obstacle, warrior. Lay them aside—know the serenity you have striven to achieve."

No longer able to fight, Camael did as he was told—and the great beast that pretended to be the voice of sanctuary—

It began to feed.

After a few more hours of small talk, Aaron was finally able to get to the computer when Mrs. Provost announced that she was going to bed. He slid the mouse smoothly across the surface of the bright blue pad and clicked on Send. "There," he said, as his e-mail disappeared into cyberspace on its way to Vilma.

"What did you say?" asked Gabriel, who rested on the floor of the cramped office.

"Nothing, really." Aaron shrugged. He began to shut the computer down. "I told her I was thinking about her and that I hope she's doing okay. Small talk—that's all."

"You like this female, don't you, Aaron?"

"I don't like to think about that stuff, Gabriel," he said, turning off the computer and leaning back in the office chair. He ran his fingers through his dark hair. "Verchiel and his goons would like nothing more than to get even with me by going after Vilma. For her own good, e-mail's the closest I'm getting for a real long time." He paused, wishing he could change things. Then he shook his head. "It's the best way."

"At least you can talk on the computer," Gabriel said, trying to be positive.

Aaron stood and switched off the light. "Yeah, I guess that's something," he said, and the two quietly left the office, making their way up to their room.

Once inside, Aaron undressed and prepared for bed. "Are you going to sleep with me or are you staying on the floor?" he asked the dog.

Gabriel padded toward the comforter on the floor and gave it a sniff. *"I think I'll sleep here tonight,"* he said as he walked in a circle before plopping himself down in the comforter's center.

Aaron pulled back the covers on the bed and crawled beneath them. "Well, if you want to come up, wake me and I'll help you."

"I'll be fine down here. This way I can stretch out and I don't have to worry about kicking you and hurting my leg."

Aaron switched off the light by the bed and said good night to his best friend. He hadn't realized how tired he was. His eyes quickly grew heavy, and he felt himself drifting away on the sea of sleep.

"What if he doesn't come back?" Gabriel suddenly asked, his words startling Aaron back to consciousness.

"What was that, Gabe?" Aaron asked sleepily.

"*Camael,*" the dog said. "*What if Camael doesn't come back? What are we going to do then?*"

It was a good question, and one that Aaron had been avoiding since the angel came up missing that afternoon. What would he do without Camael's guidance? He thought of the alien power that existed within him, and his heart began to race. "I wouldn't worry about it, pally," he said, taking his turn to be positive. "He's probably doing angel stuff somewhere. That's all. He'll be back before we know it."

"*Angel stuff,*" Gabriel repeated once, and then again. "*You're probably right,*" he said, temporarily satisfied. "*We'll see him tomorrow.*"

"That's it," Aaron said, again closing his eyes, which felt as though they'd been turned to lead. "We'll see him tomorrow."

And before he was even aware, Aaron was pulled beneath the sea of sleep, sinking deeper and deeper into the black abyss of unconsciousness, with nary a sign of struggle.

But something was waiting.

Aaron couldn't breathe.

The grip of nightmare held him fast, and no matter how he fought to awaken, he could not pull himself free of the clinging miasma of terror.

He was encased in a fleshy sack—a cocoon of some kind, and from its veined walls was secreted a foul-smelling fluid. Aaron struggled within the pouch, the milky substance rising steadily to lap against his chin. Soon it would cover his face, filling his mouth and nostrils—and he began to panic. Then he felt something in the sack with him, something that wrapped around his arms and legs, trying to keep his flailing to a minimum. Aaron knew it wanted to hold him in its constricting embrace so the fluid could immerse him completely in its foulness. His body grew numb.

"No," he cried out as some of the thick, gelatinous substance splashed into his mouth. It tasted of death, and left his flesh dulled.

He'd had similar dreams when his angelic abilities had first started to manifest. He didn't care for them then—and cared even less for them now. He intensified his battle to be free of it, but the nightmare did not relent, continuing to hold him fast in its grip.

Aaron was completely submerged now, the warm fluid engulfing him, lulling him to a place where he could quit all struggle. And it almost succeeded.

Almost.

Suddenly, in his mind, he saw a sword of light. It was the most magnificent weapon he had ever seen. Never in all his imaginings could he have built a sword so mighty and large. It was as if the weapon had been forged from one of the rays of the sun.

And as he reached for it, its unearthly radiance shone brighter, and brighter still—burning away the liquid-filled cocoon that held him and the nightmare realm it inhabited.

† † †

He awoke with a start, his body drenched with sweat. Gabriel had joined him on the bed, and his dark brown eyes glistened eerily in a strange light that danced around the room.

"Gabriel, what . . . ?" he began breathlessly.

"Nice sword," the dog said simply.

Fully awake now, Aaron realized that he held something in his left hand. Slowly he turned his gaze toward it—toward what he had brought back from the realm of nightmare.

A blade of the sun.

chapter seven

"*What* do you think it means?" Gabriel asked from the foot of the bed as Aaron stepped from the shower and grabbed a fresh shirt.

He pushed his arms through the sleeves and pulled the red T-shirt down over his stomach. "It was kind of like the dreams I had before this whole Nephilim thing blew up," he said, fingering his hair in the mirror and deciding that he looked fine. "Where I was experiencing old memories that didn't belong to me."

"*Like the sword?*" the dog asked.

Aaron shuddered as he remembered the amazing sight of the sword that he seemed to have brought over from the dream. He knew he was not responsible for the creation of the blade. He was certain that it belonged to someone of great importance, but the question was who—and why had the weapon been given to him. It had only stayed with him for a short time. As if sensing it was no longer needed, it had dispersed in an explosion of blinding light. "Just like the sword," Aaron finally replied. "And like the dreams, I think it was given to help me."

"I thought it was all very scary," Gabriel said, and sighed as he rested his snout between his paws.

"I agree," Aaron said, sitting beside the dog to put on his sneakers, "but it all has something to do with this town."

"Is this a mystery?" Gabriel asked, his floppy ears suddenly perky.

Aaron laughed and gave the dog's head a rub. "It certainly is. Listen, I've got to go to the clinic this morning, but you need to stay here and give that leg a chance to heal. Why don't you think about all our clues and see if you can come up with some answers."

"I've always wanted to solve a mystery," Gabriel said happily.

"All right there, Scooby." Aaron gave the dog another pet and headed for the door.

"Scooby?" the dog said, his head tilted at a quirky angle.

"He's a dog on television, very good at solving mysteries."

Gabriel's head tilted the other way.

"Never mind," Aaron said as he stepped out into the hall. "It's not important. I'll see you this afternoon."

"Have a good day, Shaggy," he heard the dog

say as he closed the door. And he began to laugh, marveling again at how smart his friend had actually become.

Aaron was busy at the veterinary clinic from the moment he stepped through the door. He didn't think it possible for a town so small to have that many animals in need of care. Stitches, rabies shots, heartworm tests, a broken forepaw—you name it, he and Katie dealt with it that morning and well into the afternoon.

It feels good to be working with animals again, Aaron thought as he restrained a particularly feisty Scottish terrier, by the name of Mike, who was having some blood drawn.

"No hurt! No hurt!" the little dog yelped as his owner looked on, concern in her eyes.

"It's okay," Aaron said to the dog. "When the doctor is done, you can have a cookie and go home. All right?"

The dog immediately stopped its struggling.

"That's it," Katie said, placing the vial on the counter and turning to the owner. "I'll send this out to the lab this afternoon and give you a call as soon as I know something."

Aaron handed Mike back to his owner and escorted them into the lobby to settle the bill. "And don't forget this," he said, holding out a treat as the woman turned to leave.

The woman smiled, and Mike greedily devoured the cookie.

"I never lie," Aaron said to the dog with a wink and bid them both good-bye.

"Next victim," Katie said wearily, coming out of the examination room.

For the first time that day, the waiting room was empty.

"We're good right now," Aaron told her. "Next one's"—he glanced at the appointment book—"a rabies shot at four. Gives us two hours to catch up."

"You know, you're really good with them," Katie said, leaning against the desk.

"Why, thank you, doctor," Aaron said, smiling. "I enjoy the work."

"No really, they seem to trust you. It's a talent you don't see so often."

"Well, let's just say I speak their language," he said with a grin.

Katie shook her head and looked at her watch. "You say we've got two hours before the next appointment?"

Aaron nodded.

She moved toward the door, took a ring of keys from her pocket, and locked the front door. "What's up?" he asked, a little surprised.

"Being a fellow stranger in this burg, I've got something I want to show you," she said, moving past him and down the hall. "It's in the basement."

Aaron followed her to the door at the end of the hall. There was a sudden tension in the air that hadn't been there before, and it concerned him. "Does this have anything to do with your old boyfriend?" he asked.

"Yeah," she said with a slight nod. "I think it might." She opened the door and started down the creaking wooden steps into the darkness. "Kevin contacted me, asking me to come to Blithe to help him with something, but he wasn't exactly clear as to what the problem was."

At the foot of the stairs she reached out into the inky darkness and pulled the chain for the light, dispelling the darkness to the far corners of the underground room. "So I show up and I find him missing," she continued, as she waited for Aaron to join her. "The office is in disarray. He hasn't been here for appointments for at least four days." Katie ran a trembling hand across her forehead.

Aaron's curiosity was piqued, but something was clearly upsetting Katie, and that was cause for concern.

"Yes, he was a bit of a flake, and that's part of the reason we're no longer together, but he took his job very seriously. I even went to the police to file a missing person's report, but Chief Dexter said I should give it some time—how did he put it? 'Just in case he's out sowing his wild oats.'" The vet laughed with little humor.

"What did you find, Katie?" Aaron asked quietly.

She glanced at him, then turned toward an old freezer in the corner. "First I found his journal, and it mentioned—*things* he had found in town."

"What kinds of things?"

Taking a deep breath, Katie crossed the cellar to the freezer. Aaron followed close behind her.

"Wrong things," she said, pulling open the lid on the unit. "See for yourself."

Katie reached inside the frosty innards of the freezer and withdrew a plastic bag. She let the lid slam shut, then placed the bag on top and opened it, spilling out the frozen contents. The corpse of an animal fell onto the hood with a heavy thud, and Aaron recoiled, startled and a bit repulsed. "What is it?" he whispered as he studied the frost-covered body.

It was the size of an average house cat and bore some resemblance to—of all things—a raccoon, but it wasn't either. Not really. The body was covered in long, gray fur, but the limbs were scaled, like a fish. Curved talons like that of some bird of prey grew from three of its feet— the fourth ended in a stunted tentacle.

"What is it?" Aaron asked again, unable to pull his eyes from the freakish sight.

"Your guess is as good as mine," Katie replied. She pulled a pen from her lab coat pocket and began to poke at the corpse. "This wouldn't happen to be what bit your dog, would it?"

Aaron shook his head. It was as ugly as an Orisha, but it had no connection to Gabriel's injury.

"Looks to be a little bit of everything—a real evolutionary blend." Katie shrugged and continued. "We've got some bird and rodent attributes, as well as fish—and there's also a little bit of cephalopod thrown in for good measure." She pulled the pen away and wiped it against her pants leg. "And that's just *this* one."

He looked at her hard. "There's more?" he asked uneasily.

She nodded, gesturing at the freezer. "There are at least seven others in there—each more grotesque than the last. One, *maybe* two, could pass as a random Mother Nature having a bad day—but this many?"

"What do you think it means?" Aaron asked, gazing at the monstrosity atop the freezer and imagining with disgust how the ones inside looked.

"What do I think it means?" Katie repeated. She started to put the pen back in her pocket, then seemed to think better of it and tossed it into an old barrel beside the furnace. "I think something in this town is making monsters."

Aaron and Katie hurried up the cellar steps, as if the disturbing creatures in the freezer had suddenly come to life and were chasing them. Quietly, lost in their own thoughts, they returned to the lobby, where Katie unlocked the front door.

"So you can see why I'm a little freaked," she

said, rubbing her arms with the palms of her hands as if to eliminate a winter's chill.

"Do you have any idea what's causing it?" Aaron asked, leaning against the reception desk. The memory of the previous night's dream and his run-in with the strange raccoon yesterday suddenly flooded his mind and made him flinch. *Could this somehow be connected?*

"It appears to be some kind of mutation," Katie was saying. She had walked around the desk and was pulling open the bottom drawer. She fished around inside for a moment, then removed an unopened package of Oreos. She tore open the bag and stuffed one in her mouth. "Sorry," she said, her mouth full. She offered him the bag. "I have an incredible craving for these when I'm stressed."

Aaron took a few cookies as Katie continued with her theory.

"Maybe some kind of illegal chemical dumping or drug manufacturing." Katie nibbled like a squirrel on an Oreo, eyes gazing off into space. "Something that could change an animal on a genetic level . . ."

"Here?" Aaron asked, surprised. "Is there even any industry around here big enough to cause that kind of damage?"

Katie finished her cookie and grabbed another one. "Not anymore, but there used to be a business in town that made boats. It was Blithe's major employer until it closed about fifteen years ago. The abandoned factory is still standing out by the water. Evidently the owners wanted to expand, but the land there is unstable because of underwater caves that honeycomb the coast. So they took the company to California."

"What, are you an expert on Blithe? I thought you were from Illinois." Aaron laughed, licking the crumbs from his fingertips.

Katie shrugged. "I was going to move here with Kevin before the split, so I did some research."

"You think some kind of toxic waste from the boat factory seeped into the soil?" Aaron reached for another Oreo.

"When I first came into town the other night, I got a little lost and found myself on the road that leads to the old factory." She closed up the bag and returned it to the drawer. "There was an awful lot of activity around there, especially for a place that's supposedly abandoned. I think there's something going on in Blithe, and I think my ex figured that out and that's why he's disappeared."

Aaron recalled his run-in with chief of police. *Is it paranoia talking now, or does this tiny, seaside town really have a deep, dark secret?* he wondered. But there was something—something that seemed to speak to the inhuman side of his nature. It had spoken to Camael as well, and now, like Katie's former boyfriend, he, too, was missing. "Maybe you should go to the state police," he suggested. "That would probably be the smartest thing to do, especially if you think that Kevin might have—"

Katie shook her head emphatically. "No, not yet. I've got to be sure of the details before I start making crazy accusations."

Aaron felt a knot begin to form in the pit of his stomach. "And those details are . . . ?"

"I want to check out the factory—tonight."

The knot in his gut grew uncomfortably tighter. "I'm not sure that's a good idea, Katie."

"It's the only way I can think of to prove that something's up here. Don't worry," she added with a nervous grin. "I'll be fine. I'll just poke around a little, get the evidence I need, and be back here in no time."

Alarm bells were ringing in Aaron's head, but he doubted there was anything he could say to sway the woman's resolve. The voice of reason told him he was going to seriously regret what he was about to say, but he hated the idea of Katie going alone even more. "I'll go with you," he said quickly, before he could change his mind.

Katie approached him, a look of genuine gratitude in her eyes. "You don't have to," she said, and reached out to touch his shoulder. "This is something *I* have to do, just in case Kevin—"

"No, I'm going with you," Aaron interrupted.

He shrugged. "After all, we out-of-towners have to stick together."

Before they could say any more, the door opened and a mother and two children entered with a pet carrier containing a yowling cat.

"The four o'clock, I'd guess," Aaron said, looking at his watch. "A little early."

"Thank you, Aaron." Katie looked hard into his eyes before stepping out from behind the counter to escort the family into the examination room. "What would I do without you?"

chapter eight

Gabriel awoke with a start.

He'd been dreaming about chasing a rabbit through a dense forest, weaving and ducking beneath thick bushes and low-hanging branches, when his drowsing reverie turned unexpectedly to nightmare. The rabbit had stopped and spun around to glare at him with eyes that did not seem right. They were unusually dark, almost liquid in their shininess, and when they blinked, a milky coating seemed to briefly cover them. Gabriel had seen many rabbits in his years—but never one that looked like this. It was wrong— the bunny was wrong.

Its body had begun to writhe—to undulate as if something inside of it were trying to get out. Slowly, cautiously, Gabriel had backed away, growling in his most menacing tone. The animal lay flat on the ground. Its body had continued to pulse and vibrate, its scary eyes never leaving the dog. Gabriel barked: a succession of sharp staccato bursts and snarls, hoping to scare the rabbit away. He had wanted to run, but didn't want to turn his back on the creature. *How embarrassing*, he had thought in the grip of his nightmare, *to be chased by a rabbit*.

The rabbit had suddenly stopped moving, although its unwavering gaze never left Gabriel. Slowly its mouth began to open—wider—and wider still. The dog heard a disturbing wet crack as the animal's jaw popped from its socket. He wanted to run—but he was afraid. The rabbit's lower jaw dangled awfully, its mouth a gaping chasm of darkness. From within, the sound of movement came. Gabriel had whined with fear and was turning to flee, when something exploded from the rabbit's body. . . .

Still shaken from the disturbing dream, Gabriel glanced about the room from his post atop the bed, nose twitching—searching the air for anything out of the ordinary. Everything seemed to be fine, but then he caught a whiff of something that made his mouth begin to water. Food, and if his senses could be trusted, it was meat loaf. He'd had his breakfast and half an apple before Aaron left for work, but the thought of a snack was quite alluring.

Gabriel turned to sniff at the wound on his leg. Aaron had wanted him to stay off of it, but it was feeling much better. The dog jumped to the floor and stretched the hours of inactivity from his limbs. It felt good, and he barely noticed any discomfort. He walked around the room in a circle, just to be certain. There was a little tightness in the muscles of his thigh, but nothing that could prevent him from heading downstairs for a handout.

He stood at the door and hopped up on his back legs to take the doorknob tightly in his mouth. Slowly, he turned his head, pulling ever so slightly until the door came open. Gabriel made his way down the hallway and carefully descended the stairs. At the foot of the steps, he again sniffed, pinpointed the kitchen as the source of his treat, and made a beeline for the doorway.

Mrs. Provost was sitting at the kitchen table and was about to take a bite from a meat loaf sandwich when Gabriel appeared.

"Well, look who it is," she said with a hint of a smile. She took a large bite and began to chew.

Gabriel padded into the kitchen, tail wagging, nails clicking on the linoleum floor. His eyes were fixed on the plate of food, and he licked his chops hungrily.

"Now don't go giving me the hungry horrors routine," Mrs. Provost said as she wiped her mouth with a paper napkin and looked away. "Aaron said I wasn't to give you anything, even if you came begging."

He watched closely as she took another bite

of the delicious-looking meat-and-bread combination. *How can Aaron do this to me again?* he wondered, remembering the incident at the rest stop. He felt the saliva begin to drip from his mouth and land upon the floor beneath him.

"Don't stare at me," Mrs. Provost said, finishing the last of the first half. "He was very serious, made me promise and everything, so you might as well just go on back to your room." She picked up the other half.

Gabriel was sure he'd never been so hungry, and couldn't believe the woman wouldn't share even a small piece of her sandwich. It was very selfish. Remembering his success with the little girl and her family, he reached out with his mind to reassure the woman that Aaron wouldn't be mad if he was given only a bite.

I'm sure it would be fine if you gave me a bite of that sandwich.

Mrs. Provost convulsed violently as his mind gently brushed against hers. The table shook, spilling the cup of coffee next to her plate. Gabriel stepped back, startled.

She had set her sandwich down for a moment, but picked it up again, opening her mouth to take a bite. Again, Gabriel lightly prodded, suggesting that it would be very nice of her to share. She froze and gradually turned in her chair. His tail wagged in anticipation as he came closer. But the old woman stared at him, a strange expression on her face, as if she had never seen him before. She was still holding the sandwich in her hand, and he continued to hope that he would get some of it, but a primitive instinct told him that something was wrong. He felt the hackles of fur on his back begin to rise. Quickly the dog looked about the kitchen for signs of danger, his nose twitching eagerly as he searched for a scent that was out of the ordinary. There was a hint of something, but he did not know what it was.

Mrs. Provost made a strange noise at the back of her throat, and the skin around her neck seemed to expand, like a bullfrog. And then she blinked, a slow, languid movement, and Gabriel saw that same milky covering over her eyes that he'd seen on the rabbit in his dream.

Suddenly he didn't care whether he got a bite of the meat loaf sandwich. He backed toward the doorway, never taking his eyes from the strange old woman. Her scent had changed. It was like the ocean—but older. He had to get to Aaron.

Gabriel spun around and bolted for the front door. Again, he jumped up and grabbed the knob with his teeth. He could hear sounds of the woman's approach behind him. The knob turned, and he heard the click of the latch—and another sound. The woman was coughing loudly, hard. Gabriel had just pulled the door open when he felt the first of the projectiles hit his left leg. He chanced a quick glance and saw a circular object, smaller than a tennis ball, covered in wet, glistening spines, sticking in his thigh. He wanted to pluck it out with his teeth, but feared the spines would hurt his mouth. *Aaron will get it out,* Gabriel thought as he turned back to the open door.

But Mrs. Provost was coughing again, and he felt the pricks of more barbs as they struck him. Suddenly the door seemed so very far away. *How can this be?* Gabriel wondered. He was running as fast as he could, yet he didn't seem to be going anywhere. It was all so confusing. A horrible numbness was spreading through his body, and he slumped to the floor in the doorway, his nose just catching a hint of the smells of the Maine town outside.

But there was something else that he smelled, and it came from the woman. Gabriel felt her hands roughly grab at him and drag his body back into the hallway. *It smells wrong,* he thought as he slowly drifted down into oblivion, *like something from the ocean.*

Like something bad *from the ocean.*

Aaron couldn't believe what he had committed himself to.

His thoughts raced as he let himself into Mrs. Provost's home. *I've got to be out of my mind.* But it was too late now; he had agreed to help Katie search the abandoned factory, and that was what he was going to do. *Who knows,* he thought, *maybe I'll be able to figure out why I've been feeling so strangely, or where Camael's gone, for that matter.*

"Mrs. Provost?" he called out, walking toward the kitchen. He was hoping for something to eat before his *Mission: Impossible* began. It would be just as easy to make a sandwich, but he wanted to be sure his host wasn't planning for something else. He didn't want to annoy her; something told him that would be a bad thing.

The kitchen was empty, but he noticed a plate with a half-eaten meat loaf sandwich on the table. Aaron returned to the hallway and called again. "Mrs. Provost? Are you home?"

Getting no response, he decided to go upstairs and check on Gabriel. He would need to clean the dog's wound, then feed him, and most likely make himself something to eat before embarking on his nighttime maneuvers with Katie.

"Hey, Gabriel, how you feeling, boy . . . ," Aaron said as he pushed open the door and stepped into the room. His eyes fell upon the empty bed, then went to the comforter on the floor, and he saw with a growing unease that it, too, was missing his best friend. Aaron stepped farther into the room, leaving the door open wide behind him.

"Gabriel," he called again as he peered around the bed, finding nothing. He began to panic. Maybe the dog had injured himself so badly that he'd had to be taken to the veterinarian, which would also explain the half-eaten sandwich and Mrs. Provost's absence. Aaron decided to give Katie a call, just to be sure. He turned to the doorway and stopped.

Mrs. Provost stood in the hall, just outside the door.

"You scared me," Aaron said with a surprised smile. Almost immediately he knew something wasn't right. "What's wrong?" he asked, advancing toward her. "Where's Gabriel—is he all right?"

The woman did not respond. She simply stared at him oddly with eyes that seemed much darker than they had before.

"Mrs. Provost?" he asked, stopping in his tracks. Instincts that could only be connected to the inhuman part of his identity began to scream in warning, "Is there something . . ."

The old woman's neck suddenly swelled. She bent forward, coughed violently, and expelled something toward him.

The sword from his nightmare was suddenly in Aaron's hand, and instinctively he swatted aside the projectiles. Most exploded into dust upon contact with the blade of light, but pieces of some fell to the hardwood floor, and he tried to make sense of what he saw. They looked like fat grapes, fat grapes with sharp-looking quills sticking out of them.

The old woman grunted with displeasure, a wet gurgling sound like a stopped-up drainpipe, and he saw that her throat again had begun to expand. Aaron swung the blade of white light, directing its powerful radiance toward what he had been fooled into believing was a pretty cool old woman.

"No more," he heard himself say in a voice that did not sound at all like his.

The blade's luminescence bathed Mrs. Provost in its unearthly light, and her throat immediately deflated, expelling a noxious cloud of gas. Her callused hands rose to shield her eyes against the searing light, and he saw something that chilled the blood in his veins—a second eyelid.

Aaron advanced toward her. "What are you?" he asked, his voice booming. "And where is my dog? Where is Gabriel?"

The woman crouched on the floor. His mind raced with the strangeness of it all, and he thought of the things frozen in the basement of the veterinary clinic. *Is it all connected?* he wondered, and a voice deep down inside him said that it was.

Mrs. Provost sprang from the floor, an inhuman hiss escaping her mouth as she lashed out at him, attempting to swat the blade away. The strangely sweet scent of burning flesh perfumed the air, and Aaron stumbled back, startled by the attack. The old woman screamed, but it sounded more like the squeal of an animal in pain. She threw herself from the room, clutching at her injured hand, where she had touched his weapon.

Aaron wished the awkward sword away

and ran after her. Mrs. Provost was running erratically toward the stairs, as if she was no longer in control of her motor functions. He could only watch in horror as her feet became entangled and she tripped, tumbling down the stairs in a shrieking heap.

Aaron ran down the steps as the woman's body spilled limply into the foyer. He knelt beside her and reached to touch her neck for a pulse. Her heart rate was erratic, and her hand had begun to blister, but other than that, she seemed relatively unscathed. A low, murmuring gurgle escaped from her throat, and she began to writhe upon the floor.

Aaron reached down and pried open her mouth, keeping an eye on her throat for swelling. He tilted her head slightly so that he could see into her mouth. Something in the shadows at the back of her mouth scuttled away, escaping down her throat. Disturbingly enough, based on the quick glimpse, whatever it was reminded him of a hermit crab he'd once had as a pet. He quickly took his hands away.

Something was living inside Mrs. Provost. Again, he thought of the frozen animals in the freezer back at the clinic, their bodies changed— twisted into some new and monstrous form of life. He wondered if they, too, had something hiding away inside them.

He touched the woman's chin again, pulling open her mouth slightly. *"What are you?"* he asked, hoping that by using his preternatural gift of languages he could speak to the thing hiding away inside Mrs. Provost. If it worked on dogs and other animals, why not on this?

Her body shuddered, the flesh beneath her clothes beginning to writhe.

"What are you?" he asked again, more forcefully.

It started as a grumbling rumble in what seemed to be the old woman's stomach, and he watched with increasing horror as the bulge that formed in her abdomen traveled upward, toward her chest—and then her throat. The skin of her neck expanded, and Aaron immediately backed away. He was about to summon his weapon of light when Mrs. Provost's mouth snapped open and a horrible gurgling laugh filled the air, followed by an equally chilling voice.

"What am I?" it asked in a language composed of buzzes and clicks. *"I am Leviathan. And we are legion."*

interlude three

"*C*ome," a voice boomed in the darkness, echoing through the endless void that had become his being. *"Hear my voice and come to me."*

Stevie knew not why, but he found himself responding, drawn to the powerful sound that invaded his solitude. It reverberated through his cocoon of shadow, touching him, comforting him in ways that the darkness could not.

"Oblivion shall claim you no longer."

And then there was a light, burning through the ebony pitch—and he winced, turning his face away, blinded by its awesome intensity.

"Fear not the light of my righteousness," the voice said. *"There is a powerful purpose awaiting you beyond the stygian twilight—work to be done."*

And the radiance continued to grow, consuming the darkness, pulling him from the embrace of shadow and into the heart of illumination.

"*Come to me,*" said the voice, so very close. "*And be reborn.*"

Reborn.

Verchiel knelt before he who mere moments before had been a child. Silently the Archons watched as the angel held the face of the magickally augmented boy in both hands and gazed into eyes vacant of awareness.

"Do you hear me?" he asked. "Your lord and master has need of you."

The angel examined the magnificently muscled body of the boy-turned-man, pleased with the work of his magicians. The arcane symbols that had been painted, then burned into his naked flesh, had formed permanent scars decorating the perfect physique. These were marks that would set him apart from all others; symbols that proved he had been touched by the divine, transformed into something that transcended simple humanity.

Again, Verchiel looked into the eyes of the man. "I call upon you to come forth. There is so much to be done," he whispered. Lovingly he touched the man's expressionless face, running his long, delicate fingers through the blond, sweat-dampened hair. "I have need of you," he hissed, leaning his mouth close to the man's own. "The Lord God has need of you."

Verchiel brought a hand to the man's chin, pulled open his mouth, and blew lightly into the open maw, an icy blue flame briefly illuminating the cavern of the open mouth. The body of the man, who had once been Stevie, twitched once and then was still. Verchiel continued to stare, willing the man to consciousness, a vacant shell ready to be shaped into a tool of surgical precision.

An instrument of redemption.

The man's body began to thrash, flopping about on the floor of the sunroom, and a smile languidly spread across Verchiel's pale, scarred features. "That's it," he cooed. "I'm waiting— we're all waiting."

Awareness suddenly flooded into the man's eyes, and his body went rigid with the shock of it. He began to scream, a high-pitched wail of rebirth that tapered off to a wheezing gasp as he rolled from side to side on the cold solarium floor.

Verchiel gestured toward the door, and several of his soldiers entered the room. They lifted the man, mewling and trembling, from the ground and held him aloft.

"Look at you," Verchiel said, a cold, emotionless smile on his face. "The potential for greatness emanates from you in waves." He held up a single, long, and pointed finger to the man who was crying pathetically. "But there is something missing. Something that will make you complete." He turned to the Archons, who held pieces of an armor the rich red color of spilt blood. "Dress him," the Powers' leader ordered.

And the magicians did as they were told, covering the man's body in crimson metal forged in the fires of Heaven. When they completed their task, they stepped away, and Verchiel approached. Every inch of the man's transformed flesh was encased in bloodred metal—all except his head. He was a fearsome sight in his crimson suit of war, but he gazed pathetically at Verchiel, eyes streaming tears of fear and confusion.

"It's all so new to you now," Verchiel said, holding out his hands to the man. "But I will make it right." Fire appeared between the angel's outstretched hands, at first no bigger than the flame on the head of a match, then growing into a swirling fireball of orange. "I will teach you," the angel said as the fire grew darker, taking shape, solidifying into a helmet the matching color of lifeblood. "You shall be my tool of absolution." He placed the helmet over the man's head. "My implement of absolution."

Verchiel stepped back, admiring the fearful visage standing before him, clad in the color of pulsing rage. "Malak—," he said, extending his hand, introducing those around him to the newest weapon in their arsenal. "Hunter of false prophets."

chapter nine

In the apartment above the clinic, Katie was lost in her thoughts; in a place dark and dank, loaded with hundreds of metal barrels, corroded with age, their toxic contents seeping into the groundwater, invading the ecosystem of the Maine town.

The microwave oven began to beep, and she pulled herself from the disturbing reverie to answer its insistent toll. She took the steaming mug of chicken soup from inside and sat at the little kitchenette. Her stomach felt queasy with nerves, but she knew she should eat something before her late night maneuvers.

In between spoonfuls, Katie pulled a yellow legal pad over and reviewed the list of things she would need to gather before tonight. She tapped the first item on the pad with her finger. "Flashlight," she said thoughtfully. "I saw one around here somewhere."

She got up from the chair and approached some boxes that had been neatly stacked by the doorway to Kevin's bedroom. *How long had he been here and still hadn't completely unpacked?* Katie moved some of the boxes and found the flashlight, pointed it into the room, and turned it on. Its beam cut through the encroaching shadows that accumulated with the coming of dusk.

"Guess that's a check," she said, returning to the table and setting the flashlight beside the pad. She was just about to sit, when she heard a faint knock on the door. She glanced at the clock. She was expecting Aaron, but it was only just seven. Maybe he'd come early to try to talk her out of her planned adventure. "A little early, aren't you . . . ," she began, stopping when she saw that it wasn't Aaron on the doorstep.

Blithe's chief of police stood stiffly in the doorway and stared.

"Can I help you with something, Chief?" Katie asked.

It was almost as if she'd woken him up. He kind of twitched, then politely removed his hat. "Sorry to disturb you, ma'am," he said, "but I've got some news about Dr. Wessell."

Katie felt her heart sink, as though the floor beneath her suddenly gave way and she was falling into a bottomless chasm. "What is it?" she asked in a breathless whisper, stepping aside to invite the sheriff inside.

He stepped in, and she closed the door

behind him. The silence in the room became almost deafening, and Chief Dexter nervously coughed into his hand.

"Can I get you something?" she asked as she walked farther into the kitchen, trying to delay the inevitable.

"A glass of water would be fine," he answered.

She took a glass from a cabinet and began to run the water. "You have to run it for a minute," she said offhandedly, putting her hand beneath the stream. "Takes a while to get cold."

He nodded, self-consciously turning his hat in his hands.

She handed him the glass, then leaned back against the sink and folded her arms across her chest. "Is it bad?" she finally asked.

Chief Dexter was taking a drink from his glass when he shuddered violently, as if wracked by an Arctic chill. The glass tumbled from his hand and smashed upon the floor.

"Chief?" Katie asked, moving toward him.

His eyes were closed, but he raised a hand to reassure her. "Dr. Wessell," he began, his voice sounding strange . . . raspy, "he discovered some things about our town—things that should have remained secret."

Katie was kneeling on the kitchen floor, carefully picking up the pieces of broken glass, when the implications of the police officer's words began to sink in. "What exactly are you suggesting, Chief?" she asked, slowly climbing to her feet, the palm of one of her hands piled with shards of glass. "Did someone do something to Kevin?"

She was startled by the man's response. Chief Dexter chuckled, and it was one of the most unpleasant sounds she'd ever heard—like his throat was clogged with fluid—and it must have been a trick of the light, but something seemed to be wrong with his eyes. "He serves the whole—as do we all," he said dreamily, and began to sway from side to side.

Katie was suddenly afraid—very, very afraid. Something wasn't right with the man; something wasn't right with the whole damn town. "I think you had better leave now," she said in her calmest voice. *He serves the whole,* she thought. *What the hell is that supposed to mean?*

"Get out," she said, turning her back on him defiantly and walking to the trash can beside the sink to dispose of the glass in her hand. She didn't want him to know that he'd spooked her. Never show fear; it was something she'd learned in her work with animals. Even still, she kept an especially large shard of glass in her hand—just in case she needed to defend herself, but as she turned she saw that he was walking toward the door.

"Can't have people poking around," he said in that wet, gravelly voice as he reached the door and opened it. "Not when we're so close to being free."

Katie had no idea what the man was talking about and was ready to rush the door and lock it behind him. But the chief just opened the door and stepped back inside, as if waiting for somebody to join him.

This is it, she thought, and dove across the room for the phone. She would try the state police. Their number was on the yellow legal pad she left on the kitchen table. Katie squeezed the razor sharp piece of glass in her hand as she moved in what seemed like slow motion across the kitchen, the pain of the shard digging into her flesh keeping her focused.

From the corner of her eye she saw the policeman begin to crouch. Was he going for his gun? Katie reached out for the handset. *Just a bit farther.*

She collided with the circular kitchen table, almost dislocating her hip, and was reaching for the phone when she heard the noise. Not the sound of a gunshot—but the sound of a cough, a violent hacking sound.

Her hand was on the receiver when she felt it hit her neck, something that made her skin burn as if splashed with acid. Reflexively her hand went to her neck, and she pulled the object from her flesh. It reminded her of a sea urchin, black and glistening, its circular shape covered in sharp spines—but where did it come from? She could feel the numbness spreading from her neck to her body with incredible speed.

Katie looked toward the sheriff by the open door just as he let loose with another of the powerful coughs. A spray of projectiles spewed from his mouth to decorate her body, and she realized with increasing horror that she could not feel a thing. She held up her hand, the one holding the piece of shattered glass, and watched, almost amused as the blood continued to flow from the cuts, running down her arm to spatter upon the floor.

She felt as though she were in a dream, the world around her suddenly not making sense. Katie glanced down at the urchins attached to her flesh. *They must be coated in some kind of poison*, she gathered as she toppled to the floor, banging her head on the edge of the table.

Katie lay facing the open door. The sheriff still stood beside it. She wanted to scream, but all she could do was lie there and watch him as he stood, like a doorman, waiting for someone to arrive.

She heard the sounds of claws scrabbling on the wooden steps outside. It didn't sound like a person at all, she mused, but like an animal having some difficulty making it up the steps.

"We're so very close," Chief Dexter said, looking toward the door with anticipation. "Nothing must prevent the *whole* from being free."

Again there was the comment about the whole, and she wrestled with the meaning as she fought to keep the numbed lids over her eyes from sliding closed. She had to see what was coming up the steps, had to see what the sheriff so eagerly awaited.

It made its appearance, lurching across the

doorframe and into the apartment with great difficulty. Katie knew that she had lost the ability to scream some time ago, but it didn't prevent her from trying, as a monstrosity very similar to the ones dead in the basement freezer came toward her. It was the most horrible thing she'd seen in her life, a thing of nightmare; its body made up of attributes of many other animals, but having no identity of its own. A beaver, a snake, an octopus, a crane, and even a fish; all were represented in the horrific mass that shambled across the kitchen floor. The monster had a great deal of difficulty with the tile floor; one of its back limbs, a clawed flipper, sliding across the smooth surface not allowing it purchase. It smelled of low tide, and she silently wished that her sense of smell had been numbed as well.

Blithe's chief of police knelt beside the abomination. "To keep the secret," he said in a soft gurgle, "you must serve the whole." He reached down and began to stroke the fur, scales, and feathers that grew from the body of the grunting beast. "You must be made part of the whole."

Katie was suddenly filled with an overwhelming sense of dread as her eyes grew unbearably heavy and began to close. She saw the animal begin to shiver, its twisted mouth opening as if it was having trouble breathing. Then, mercifully, her eyes shut upon the nightmarish visage before her. Katie listened to the wheezing and grunting beast, the smell of the tide washing over her as it gasped for breath.

And then she heard a sound that at first she could not identify. It was a sharp sound, one that would have made her flinch if she hadn't been under the effects of a toxin—a ripping sound— followed by the sound of something spilling, something splashing onto the floor.

"Part of the whole," she heard Dexter say softly in the darkness, as the sound of something on many legs skittered across the tiled floor toward her.

As she slipped further, deeper into oblivion, she felt it touch her.

"Dear God," echoed her last thought as she surrendered to the poisons coursing through her veins. *"It's crawling into my mouth."*

Aaron had no idea what he would find, as he cautiously climbed the wooden steps that led to Kevin Wessell's apartment. He'd called both the clinic and the apartment, but Katie hadn't answered at either place. That awful feeling of dread, which he had become a little too familiar with of late, churned in the pit of his stomach.

The thing living inside Mrs. Provost had continued to rant about something called Leviathan and how the *whole* would soon be free. He had no idea what it was talking about, and finally locked the woman in the basement. There really wasn't much of a choice, he had to find Gabriel and Camael, and make sure that Katie was all right.

The apartment door was unlocked, and he opened it into the kitchen, knocking lightly as he stuck his head inside. "Katie?" he called out. The lights were on, and everything seemed normal until he noticed the splatters of blood on the floor near the kitchen table. There was another puddle of something on the floor near the blood-stains, and he knelt down beside it. It was clear, gelatinous, and he touched it with the tips of his fingers, bringing it to his nose. It smelled strong, reminding him of Lynn Beach during low tide: a kind of nasty, rotten-egg stink.

Aaron wiped the slimy substance on his pant leg and explored the kitchen further. He found the legal pad with Katie's list and the flashlight on the table. She must have been getting ready to go to the abandoned boat factory.

The factory.

He took the flashlight from the table and tested it. The factory seemed as good a place as any to continue the search for his missing friends. He doubted it was anything as simple as a toxic spill cover-up—the thing living inside Mrs. Provost had told him that much. Of course, that's just the way things were lately; nothing was normal—or easy.

Aaron headed into the night, taking the flashlight with him. He and Katie had discussed how to get to the factory earlier in the day, and he thought he could find his way. Keeping mostly to the shadows, he proceeded through the winding side street to the docks. The going was creepy. There wasn't a sign of life anywhere; every house he passed was shrouded in darkness. He began to wonder how many citizens of Blithe had one of those things, like the one in Mrs. Provost, living inside of them. He shuddered, an uncomfortable tightness forming in his throat.

It wasn't long before he could hear the sound of the ocean and smell the tang of the salt air. Aaron crept from the wooded area and down a sandy embankment to a lonely stretch of road ending in a high, chain-link fence. He could just about make out the shape of the factory beyond it.

A light approached from the opposite direction, and Aaron ducked for cover, watching the road from behind a sprawling patch of wildflowers and tall grass. The Ford pickup truck slowed as it approached the fence, and Aaron watched the driver slowly climb out. With a key from his pocket, he unlocked a padlock and chain, pushing open the fence to allow the vehicle entrance. Though it was dark, Aaron could see that the back of the truck was filled with people: young and old; men, women, and children; some even dressed in their pajamas and bathrobes. With a chilling resonance, his questions about the townsfolk became horribly clear.

The driver locked the chain again after driving through, then continued on toward the factory. Its headlights illuminated the parking area, and Aaron noticed that the lot was nearly full.

Must be the night shift, he thought as he emerged from hiding, hugged the shadows, and squeezed himself between the gates and onto the property. Using the parked cars as cover, Aaron made his way closer to the factory. Some cars had been parked at the front of the sprawling building, their lights on and pointed toward the structure for illumination. He ducked lower as a police patrol car slowly came around the corner. Peeking out over the hood of a powder blue Volvo, Aaron saw that the car was driven by Chief Dexter, and waited until the policeman had driven around the building before attempting to get any closer.

Aaron watched the group that had been in the back of the pickup stiffly walk from the parking lot toward the factory. A small town with a secret, mysterious disappearances, the locals acting strangely; if he wasn't currently living it, he'd think he had become trapped in a bad sci-fi movie. They entered the building through a large, rust-stained metal door, and Aaron could hear the staccato rattle of what could only be a jackhammer.

He didn't want to chance being noticed, so he avoided the main entrance and sought another, less obvious way into the factory. He stayed close to the building's side, the shadows thrown by the rundown structure serving well to hide him. He was exceptionally cautious of Chief Dexter's patrol, remaining perfectly still in the darkness and holding his breath whenever the squad car passed.

He found what seemed to be an old emergency exit and tried to open it. No good; it was locked from the other side. "Damnit," he hissed. He looked around for something he could use to force the door, but there was nothing. Besides, he didn't want to attract any attention. He needed to get inside. *C'mon, Aaron. Think.*

And then it dawned on him. It was a wild idea, but the more he thought about it, the more he was convinced that it just might work. Aaron closed his eyes and thought of a weapon—a weapon of fire. It was a different experience than the other times that he had summoned a fiery blade; he was not being attacked in any way, so he wondered if it would even work. The blade of light, brought forth from his recent nightmare, immediately surged into his head, as if eager to be used yet again, but he deemed it too large and unwieldy for the more delicate task he had in mind. Aaron pictured a dagger with a long, thin blade, and he opened his eyes to see it begin to form in his hand.

"Would you look at that," he whispered as the knife took shape. Maybe he wasn't such a lost cause after all, he mused as he brought the glowing manifestation of his power to the door and ran the orange blade between the jamb and the door itself. There was the slightest bit of resistance as the knife dissolved the locking mechanism, the pungent aroma of melting metal wafting up into the air on tufts of oily smoke.

He gave the door a sharp tug, and it opened enough for him to slip inside. It was cool, damp, and completely void of light. Aaron wished the tool of fire away and turned on the flashlight he had stuck in his back pocket. He was in a cinderblock hallway that appeared to be used for storage; every piece of old equipment, desks, chairs, and just general crap were piled inside. Silently, he scrambled over the piles of junk, heading for a doorway on the other side, listening intently for sounds of activity outside.

Aaron got to the other side and proceeded down a shorter hallway. The sounds of machinery were louder now; the whine of gas-powered generators, the roar of heavy machinery, the *beep-beep-beep* of vehicles backing up. He quickened his pace, then stopped in the shadows of another doorway, staring in awe. If this had once been a factory, a place where people had come to work, to make things—sailboats, in fact—it certainly wasn't anymore. Inside the factory, in the middle of the sprawling structure, was an enormous hole.

Aaron skulked closer, using piles of dirt and

rock that had been stacked in huge mounds around the dig as cover, and peered over the lip of the hole. The citizens of Blithe were working deep inside, using all kinds of construction equipment to make the opening even bigger. He actually recognized people from the town: the Mainiac with his dirty Red Sox cap, and an older woman who had been in the veterinarian's office with a sick parakeet. The people down below moved around like ants, using picks, shovels, and jackhammers, chopping and digging in areas too small for the bigger machinery, while others carted away wheelbarrows loaded with the rubble of their labors.

This is way too much, he thought. He wanted nothing more than to find Gabriel and Camael and get the hell outta Dodge, but he couldn't do that; he couldn't leave Katie, and he couldn't leave the town in the thrall of Leviathan—whatever the heck that was. He wished his mentor was there; he could have used a little guidance from the angel warrior.

He recalled something that Katie had mentioned about underground caves and tunnels beneath the factory and wondered if they were the reason for this frantic activity. As if compelled, he moved cautiously closer, descending some makeshift stairs that took him deeper into the hole. There were lights strung along the walls, about every five feet or so, and the shadows cast by the workers, as they tirelessly toiled, were eerily disturbing—the distorted versions of themselves upon the tunnel wall more a reflection of the twisted horrors that lived inside them.

At the foot of the stairs he found an entrance to a tunnel, whose edges were not jagged and rough like those hewn with the tools and machines. Flashlight in hand, and making sure that he was not being watched, Aaron darted through the opening and began a descent farther beneath the earth. The walls of the winding passage were strangely smooth, as if polished— *maybe by the flow of the ocean at one time,* he thought as he placed his hand against the cool rock. It still felt wet, cold, as if the sea had left the essence of itself behind. There was a downward pitch to the tunnel floor, and Aaron nervously wondered how many feet beneath the surface he had traveled. This thought was quickly discarded when the angry sound of something squealing wafted up from the passage ahead.

It was an animal frantically calling for help, and Aaron slowly, carefully, made his way down the declining passageway. He came to a sudden, sharp bend and warily peered around it. The tunnel split, one path veering off to the left, winding down even farther into the darkness, the other ending in a chamber from where he was sure the sounds of distress had come. The animal's squeals of protest became even more frantic and Aaron was drawn closer to its plight.

He cautiously peeked into the chamber and found a makeshift veterinary office. A table, probably from the factory's cafeteria, had been set up as an examination table in the center of the room, and a man, his clothing caked with dirt, was in the process of pulling a large cat from one of many pet carriers stacked around the cave. The carriers held all manner of four-legged creatures—cats, dogs, rabbits—and Aaron checked them all for a sign of Gabriel. But his best friend was not among those imprisoned.

The filthy man had the yowling, long-haired cat by the scruff of its neck and brought it to the table. The other animals had begun to yelp and whine, knowing something bad was about to happen. The man strapped the squirming feline to the table and began to examine it, roughly checking its ears, eyes, and then inside its hissing mouth. *Could this be the missing Kevin Wessell?* Aaron wondered as the man left the cat and moved out of his line of vision.

A strange mewling cry, the likes of which Aaron had never heard before, filled the cave. The man returned to the examination table, his arms full, and Aaron had to blink twice before his mind could adjust to what he saw. It was one of the . . . *things* that Katie had shown him in the basement freezer—only this one was alive, cradled gently in the man's arms. The animals in the chamber howled and clawed at the walls of their cages. The cat thrashed against its restraints and spat as the man set the abomination down next to it. The twisted animal looked as though it might have, at one time, been a dog—a terrier of some kind, maybe—but now it was horribly more than that.

The man had begun to pet the awful beast, his filth-encrusted hand stroking the beast repeatedly from the top of its misshapen head to the patch of bare, pink flesh in the small of its back. His attention to the animal was growing rougher, more frantic, when Aaron noticed the bulbous growth forming within the barren swath of skin.

The cacophony of animal wails was almost deafening, and Aaron wanted to look away. The poor beasts knew what was about to happen, and it brought them to the brink of madness. The angelic nature residing within him suddenly began to stir; it, too, sensed the potential for danger here, and was attempting to assert itself.

The swollen mass on the creature's back had more than doubled in size and was pulsing with a life all its own. The monstrous animal panted with exertion as the tumor continued to grow, and the man looked on with a dull expression of disinterest, as if he saw things like this every day.

Suddenly the flesh of the beast's back exploded with a faint pop, and a geyser of fluid shot into the air. What Aaron saw next chilled him to the bone. As the fluid drained from the ruptured growth, something emerged from the hollow of the wound. It was spiderlike, crablike. He'd never seen anything quite like it, but was certain that this was what had been lurking in the back of Mrs. Provost's throat. It was black and glistening, the chitinous shell that covered its body catching the light of the Coleman lanterns placed around the cavern. The creature crawled from the open wound of the animal's back and scrambled onto the tabletop.

The caged animals barked, howled, and screeched in protest as the spidery thing approached the restrained feline. Aaron could understand their intensifying terror, but had to ignore their frantic cries, for there was nothing he could do. The cat didn't have a chance. In what seemed like the blink of an eye, he watched the multilimbed life-form throw itself at the cat's face and force its way into the panicked animal's mouth, disappearing down its throat. The cat thrashed and coughed, but in a matter of seconds the panic halted, and the cat relaxed, lying perfectly still, its large, bushy tail languidly waving in the air. He could have sworn he heard it purring.

His mind raced as he wrestled with what he should do, but the decision was put on hold when he heard the sound of his name being whispered.

"*Aaron*," the voice hissed in the tunnel behind him, and he backed away from the cavern and turned the corner to see Katie coming closer. His finger immediately went to his lips, urging her to be silent.

She smiled at him strangely, and he felt the hair at the back of his neck suddenly stand on end. Something wasn't right, and he found the sword of light suddenly in his hands—just as her throat bulged and a spray of the grapelike objects spewed from her open mouth. He swatted them away and watched with unease as Katie recoiled violently from the blade's light. The idea of one of those spidery things crawling inside her mouth made him feel sick to his stomach, but he stood his ground, sword aloft, waiting for the next attack.

There was movement in the tunnel behind her, and the people of Blithe moved through in a wave, pushing past Katie to get at him. The angelic essence inside him roared to be free, but he could not unleash that kind of power against these people—they weren't responsible for their actions.

Aaron waved the blade in front of them, hoping to drive them back, hoping to buy himself enough time to flee deeper into the tunnel system—but there were too many, and they were much too fast. The citizens of Blithe were upon him. He had no room to maneuver, no room to block the spiny objects that erupted from their mouths. And the power that resided at his core bellowed its frustration as a rain of projectiles pierced his flesh, clinging to his cheek, his neck, and the backs of his hands—and the numbing effects of the toxin began to course through his blood.

"I will not hurt them," he said stubbornly to the angry power, and the residents of Blithe swarmed upon him, bringing him down to the tunnel floor.

And the power that was his birthright resigned itself to its fate, and allowed the darkness of unconsciousness to enfold them in its welcoming embrace.

chapter ten

$\mathfrak{T}$he tide rolled in with a soothing rumble, rushing up to greet him, flowing around his bare legs like eager lapdogs excited to make his acquaintance. Aaron gazed out over the vast expanse of the Atlantic Ocean, watching the seabirds ride the gentle breeze, and felt a peace that he had not known in quite some time.

"It's beautiful here, isn't it, Aaron?" asked a young voice.

Aaron looked down to see Stevie sitting in the sand beside him. The boy had a plastic pail and shovel and was busily digging a hole in the wet ground.

Aaron glanced into the hole and saw that it was far deeper and larger than he had first imagined. *I'll bet there are tunnels under here,* he thought for some reason. *Miles and miles of tunnels.*

"Did you hear me, Aaron?" Stevie asked,

drawing his attention away from the hole.

Aaron looked into the boy's expectant face. "I'm sorry, Stevie," he said. "I guess I zoned out for a minute there."

The little boy was only wearing a pair of bright red swim trunks, and Aaron could see that he was getting sunburned. *If we aren't careful, he thought, the kid'll get sunstroke—just like that time when* . . .

"I just said how beautiful it is here, that's all," Stevie interrupted his train of thought. The child continued to work at his hole. "I don't ever want to leave."

Aaron laughed as he knelt down beside the boy. The surf flowed over his bare feet, so warm. "We have to go home sometime," he said as he ruffled the boy's blond hair. "Don't you want to see Mom and Dad again?"

Stevie turned and pointed up the beach. "They're over there," he said. "I can see them anytime I want."

Aaron looked up and saw Lori and Tom Stanley sitting in beach chairs beneath a large, yellow umbrella, a red and white cooler between them.

They'd bought Dr Pepper, he unexpectedly recalled, the first and last time they had ever used the red and white cooler. Something had been left inside it after the beach trip, and it had spoiled, leaving behind a nasty odor. They were never able to get the smell out of it, so they'd thrown the cooler away. Aaron tried to remember how long ago that had been. It was the same trip that Stevie got sunstroke.

Lori and Tom waved happily from their beach chairs, and Aaron tentatively waved back, suddenly overcome with a sadness he couldn't comprehend.

"Don't feel sad," his foster brother said, filling his pail with sand. "There's nothing to be sad about here."

"How did you know I was feeling sad?" Aaron asked.

Stevie did not answer, and continued to dig in his hole—making it larger, deeper.

Aaron stood and gazed out over the ocean. Dark clouds were forming off in the distance— perhaps a storm coming in. "This all seems so familiar," he said, more to himself than to Stevie, as the wind ruffled his dark hair.

"And is that so bad?" the boy asked.

Aaron glanced at his little brother and saw that Gabriel now sat beside the child, tail wagging as Stevie patted his head. "Hello, Gabriel," Aaron said to the dog.

The dog wagged his tail in response, panting happily. He had been running in the water and was soaking wet, sand sticking to the fur on his legs.

"What's the matter with you, Aaron?" the child asked. "Everything here is so perfect—so peaceful. Just let yourself accept it."

The sky was darkening as the clouds drifted closer to the shore.

"I want to," Aaron replied, a feeling of pure joy beginning to bubble up within him, but he forced it back. "I really, really do—but this feels wrong. Like I lived it before."

"But you were happy then, right? And you can be that way again. It's a gift for all you've had to endure." Stevie was suddenly standing in the middle of the hole he had been digging. "Let me take your pain away." He stretched his sunburned arms toward his older brother, a smile on his face.

It seems simple enough, Aaron thought as he watched the gray clouds billow offshore. They seemed to be changing direction, leaving the sky over his head perfect, unblemished by the storm. All he need do is accept this time, this place, as his reality, and everything would be fine.

But it wouldn't.

"This is all wrong," he said aloud with a furious shake of his head. He gestured to the ocean and the world beyond it. "This isn't right, this moment has passed. It's a memory from three years ago."

"Stop it, Aaron," Stevie demanded. "Don't spoil what I've made for you."

Aaron stared at the angry child as the clouds again tumbled in from the sea, low and dark, pregnant with storm. A distant, threatening rumble of thunder shook the air. "This is all a dream—a nightmare, really."

"Aaron!" the boy screamed, stomping his foot.

"What are you?" Aaron asked, a powerful wind suddenly whipping at his clothes. "Stevie never talked like this—he barely talked at all." Aaron looked at the dog, who continued to wag his tail happily even though the wind was blowing sand into his lolling mouth. "And this isn't Gabriel. It just looks like him." Aaron stepped closer to the child. "I'll ask you again," he said grimly. "What are you?"

It was suddenly black as night on the beach, and arcs of lightning coursed across the sky as thunderclaps boomed. The ocean had been whipped into a frenzy by the tempest, with waves crashing violently on the shore.

"You can be happy again!" the child shrieked over the storm. "All you need do is—"

"What. Are. You?" Aaron spat. From the corner of his eye he could see the ocean waters, in the distance, begin to froth and boil.

"I have existed since the fifth day of creation," Stevie said in a chilling voice not his own.

Something moved beneath the roiling waters. Something large.

"I was that spark of uncertainty in the Creator's thoughts as He forged the world—that brief moment of chaos—before Genesis."

A monster emerged from the depths of the sea, skin blacker than the darkness that now surrounded them. It seemed to be at least a hundred feet tall, its wormlike body swaying above the storm-ravaged sea. Hundreds of tentacles of varying degrees of thickness and length grew from its body, writhing in the air as if desperate to entwine something in their embrace. Aaron could not pull his eyes away from the nightmarish visage as it undulated across the thrashing sea toward the beach.

"The darkness of the ocean became my dwelling," said the thing that resembled his brother. "And there I thrived, hidden beneath the waves—until the Lord God sensed my greatness and sent His angelic messengers to snuff out my glorious light."

The monster was closer now. Large, opaque sacks dangled hideously from its glistening body, swaying like pendulums as it lurched closer to land.

Aaron was unable to take his eyes from the horribly awesome sight, surprised that he could even think, let alone speak. "You're so wonderful that God decided to take you out?"

The Stevie-thing ignored his question. "The ocean was my domain, and any who dared traverse it were subject to my wrath—and I soon developed a taste for the lives of those the Creator sent to destroy me."

The enormous sea beast loomed above Aaron. Even from this distance, he could see that its mass was covered in rows of fine scales that glistened with the colors of the rainbow. If it weren't so outright hideous, he might have found it beautiful. There was a blinding flash of

lightning, followed by an explosion of thunder—
and the pregnant clouds opened up in a deluge
of thick, driving rain.

"That's what has kept me alive over the millennia, and what will eventually free me from
my prison beneath the sea."

The viscous torrents coated Aaron's body,
forcing him down upon the sand. The ground
could not absorb the thick, milky fluids, and
they pooled around him, ever rising.

The beast reached the shore, hundreds of
tiny muscular appendages propelling the nightmare up onto the beach. "I sense in you a power
that both frightens—and excites," the monster
said, its voice now coming from two places, his
little brother and the thing upon the shore, a perverse stereo effect echoing through the air.
"Never have I encountered one such as you."

Aaron fought to stand, but he felt the ground
beneath him shift, rising up to hold him fast. The
foul rain continued to fall, coating his body in a
layer of slime. "What is this place?" he frantically asked the doppelgänger of his brother.

"It could have been your individual paradise," the entity explained, its voice a disgusted
rumble. "Like a bee to the flower, I used the
promise of personal heaven to lure you to me. A
place where you would have been content until
your final days." Stevie shook its head in disappointment. "But you have rejected it."

"It's not real," Aaron spat, attempting to

voice reverberate in his mind, his head beginning to sink below the surface. He tried to scream, to bellow his belief that this was all some twisted mind manipulation, but it was cut short—abruptly silenced as a mixture of the sand, and the slime that fell in torrents from the black sky, flowed into his mouth and down his throat. *You within the belly of the beast,* the monster had gurgled.

Food for Leviathan.

The beast that was Leviathan reclined its massive shape against the cramped confines of the cave wall, where it had been trapped for countless millennia. The monster was content for now, for many of the digestive sacks that dangled from its body were filled with angelic life— brimming with power that would bring the dark deity to eventual release.

Its latest feed—the half-breed—the Nephilim, fought mightily to be free of Leviathan's hungry embrace, his mind filled with panic.

"Your struggles are futile." The monster wormed its way into Aaron's frenzied thoughts. "Take comfort in knowing that the power that resides within you—now flowing into me—will be used to reshape the world. Through the eyes of my minions I have seen what the Creator's world has become: a place teetering daily on the brink of chaos."

Leviathan showed the young man within its

belly disturbing images of the world at large. Scenes of war, wanton violence, and death flashed before the Nephilim's mind's eye, a world seemingly touched by madness.

"This is what *God* has done," the beast growled. "*I* can do better. When I am finally free from my prison beneath the earth and sea, I will use your power, your marvelous strength, to push this place toward pandemonium. And then I shall mold it in my glorious image."

Thousands of Leviathan's black-shelled spawn writhed eagerly beneath the protective cover of its scales. It would be they that would carry out the will of the beast, changing and twisting the existing fauna—from the inside out. The idea of being unleashed upon the planet made them chitter in happy anticipation.

The Nephilim continued to fight, refusing to allow the digestive nutrients to begin the process of his absorption. This annoyed the great beast, and again, it delved into the captive's mind. Indelicately it tore into his memories, and found the recollection of a life most mundane— or it was, until the power of Heaven inside his frail human shell awakened to pursue some long-forgotten, ancient prophecy of redemption.

Leviathan had no time for prophecy; it had a world to conquer.

The one called Aaron thrashed and bucked as Leviathan picked unmercifully through his memories. The beast saw the awakening of the angelic nature, the resurrection of his pet—imbibing the lowly animal with a life-force that it was currently finding most delicious—the death of his parental guardians, and the furious battle with the leader of the Powers' host, Verchiel.

The monster writhed within its prison of rock. Long had it anticipated Verchiel, and those who followed him, to seek out and attempt to eradicate the glory that was Leviathan in the name of God—but it never came to be. For some reason, it had been spared this attack. Leviathan continued to exist, feeding on prey that would allow it to survive, drawing those of an angelic nature to it. Like the cunning anglerfish, the sea beast psychically dangled the tantalizing promise of bliss before the pathetic creatures of Heaven, and it was only a matter of time before they were ensnared, resting inside its ravenous digestive sacks.

When it was finally able to emerge from its underground prison, Verchiel and the Powers would need to be dealt with. And they would feel the ferocity of Leviathan's wrath and know its insatiable hunger.

The picture of a small child—the Nephilim's sibling—flashed within the monster's mind. It was the boy-child it had used to bring the Nephilim here to Blithe. But the Nephilim saw through the ruse, and attempted to free himself—unsuccessfully.

Leviathan would do everything in its power to keep the half-breed as his own. The life-force within him was strong, intoxicating, and it would serve the behemoth well in its eventual dominion of the world.

It could sense that the Nephilim was thinking of the child again—the child in the clutches of Verchiel. This agitated the Nephilim, made him struggle all the more, interrupting the pleasures of the digestive process. Leviathan was annoyed, and again forced his way into the angelic being's thoughts. It would need to assure the youth that any hope of rescuing his brother from the clutches of the Powers was futile.

"Give up," said Leviathan to the Nephilim. "Your struggles are all for naught."

The great beast painfully recoiled, the mental activity of the angelic being frantically struggling within one of his many bellies, causing renewed discomfort.

In the youth's mind there was a thought, an image of a blinding light, a light so bright that it could pierce even the most infinite of stygian depths. And the light, that horrible, searing light, had begun to take shape, becoming something that filled the ancient deity with a feeling of dread.

The light in the Nephilim's mind had become a weapon, a weapon Leviathan had not seen since the fateful battle that had trapped it in the underground cavern.

The light had become a sword—the sword of God's messenger.

Aaron was drowning.

He tried with all his might to fight it, to keep the foul liquid from inside his body, but there was a voice, a calm, soothing voice that attempted to convince him that this was the wrong thing to do, that the fight would only prolong his pain.

Then the silky smooth tones inside his head, which promised him the end to his suffering if he would only give up, told him that his little brother was dead, that the angel Verchiel had destroyed the child soon after he was taken, that the fight was all for nothing.

And there was the overpowering sorrow of this knowledge, combined with the weighty sadness he had already been carrying: the death of his parents, being forced to flee the life he'd built for himself—to leave Vilma—it was all too painful. He had almost started to believe that it was best for him to submit, to allow the milky solution to fill his mouth and flow into his lungs.

But then the sword was there—the mysterious weapon seemingly forged from the rays of the sun, piercing the darkness of his innermost misery, burning away the shroud of sorrow and despair that enveloped him to reveal the truth.

The truth.

Aaron screamed within the membranous sack, expelling the foul liquids that had managed to find their way into his body. The sword was in his hand, as it had been that night in his dream, glowing like the new dawn, revealing the true nature of the nightmare that had taken him captive. He drew back the sword of light and cleaved his way through the fleshy, elastic wall of his prison. In his mind he heard a scream—the shriek of a monster in pain.

The fluid immediately began to drain from the open cut in the digestive organ, and he was able to breathe. The stench of the air within the sack was foul, but it was what his aching lungs craved nonetheless. He gulped greedily at the fetid atmosphere, like a man dying of thirst, coughing up remnants of the invasive liquid.

The fleshy chamber, in which he was still imprisoned, began to buck and sway, bellows of rage and pain thundering around him.

He had to get out, to escape the grabbing, organic confines, and he threw himself at the gash he had cut into it. It was what he imagined birth to be—squeezing his head through the slice, which had, miraculously, already begun to heal. Aaron tumbled from the wound, falling a great distance, before landing upon a floor of solid rock with a jarring thud. Stars exploded before his eyes, and for a moment he thought he might lose consciousness, but he shook it off, scrambling to stand, the weapon of light still in hand.

He looked around and saw that he was in a vast, underground cavern. The place was eerily quiet except for the distant thrum of the pounding surf. Thick patches of a luminescent fungus grew on the walls, throwing a sparse and eerie green light about the sprawling cave.

The blow came from behind. His mind likened it to the approach of a freight train, hitting him with such force that he was thrown through the air to land against a far wall. His head was ringing, and the bones of his back and legs screamed their protest as he struggled to regain his footing. He was bleeding from a dozen places, but still managed to hold on to the sword of light and brandished it as he fought to stand erect.

"The sword of the messenger," something bellowed from within the darkness of the cave, and then it leaned toward him, revealing itself, its tubular body so large, it was barely able to move. "I would have thought it impossible for one such as you to wield a weapon so mighty."

Though his body continued to protest, Aaron held the blade tighter as the black-scaled monster loomed above him. He studied the details of the creature that could only be Leviathan. Its body was covered in fine, interconnecting scales, like chain mail, and it swayed snakelike above him. Repulsed, Aaron could see things living beneath its body armament, familiar spidery things that would have liked nothing better than to crawl down the throats of every living thing upon the planet.

It lashed out at him with a tentacle as thick as a tree trunk, and Aaron scrabbled quickly over the cave floor. It was like the deafening crack of the world's largest bullwhip, the fleshy appendage fragmenting the rock where he once had stood.

Leviathan shifted its great size within the cavern to follow Aaron's progress, the top of its head rubbing against the ceiling as it attempted to maneuver its enormous mass in the confining space. "Where are you going, Nephilim?" it asked in its horrible, thunderous voice. "You cannot escape me. Surrender to the inevitable."

Some of the black-shelled spider things fell from the monster's body and eagerly scuttled across the cave floor to get at him. The blade of the messenger—as Leviathan had called it— made short work of the crawling things.

As he dispatched the spawn of the monster, something began to bother him. Since awakening within the digestive sack of the monster, he had not felt the presence of his angelic power. As he destroyed more of Leviathan's pets, he tried to remember when last he had felt the force, always so eager to be unleashed. It had been back in the tunnels, when he had been attacked by Katie McGovern and the residents of Blithe. It had screamed to be free and he had rebuked it, pushing it away as he had done since that first battle with the angel Verchiel.

Leviathan squirmed its bulk closer. Had the great monster somehow sucked it away? Aaron wondered as another of the Leviathan's tentacles reached down to ensnare him in its grasp. He swung at the muscular appendage, and it recoiled from the blade, hovering in the air before him like a cobra waiting for its opportunity to strike.

"Where are you?" he whispered to the presence that should have stirred inside him. "I really could use your help around now," Aaron said, alert as the monster's tentacle again attacked. There was no answer, and Aaron felt a wave of despair wash over him as he threw his diminishing strength into fighting the plentiful appendages that reached for him. He brought the blade down and watched as it dug deep into the black, muscular flesh of the beast.

"Yarrrrggghhhh," Leviathan roared as it violently pulled the injured limb away—and with it, the sword of the messenger. Aaron watched dumbfounded as the tentacle thrashed, dislodging the annoyance—sending it hurling across the cave, far from his reach, where it disappeared in a blinding flash. Panic set in. *Without any contact with the angelic nature, is it still possible for me to defend myself?* he wondered frantically.

He pressed his back to the cave wall and attempted to conjure a weapon of his own creation. Aaron breathed a sigh of relief as a blade of fire, puny in comparison with the splendor of the sword of the messenger, began to form in his hand. At least that power had not been taken from him.

Leviathan wasted no time and again attacked. The behemoth twisted within the confines of the cave, bringing its enormous mass down toward Aaron. The sword of flame sprang fully to life in his grasp, and he was raising the blade to defend himself against this latest onslaught, when his attention fell upon the many, fleshy sacks that hung obscenely from the front of the descending beast.

Aaron froze as he stared into the contents of the sea beast's numerous stomachs: the missing Camael, his poor Gabriel, one of the ugly little creatures that had attacked them on their way to Blithe—and so many others, all trapped within the bellies of the beast. The horror of it all was almost too much for him to stand.

"The sight of me—of my magnificence—it fills you with wonder," Leviathan said, reaching down to claim Aaron as its own.

Its writhing body shifted, and a rain of tentacles fell from above to ensnare him. Aaron slashed at the relentless onslaught, the fiery weapon severing many of the limbs. The beast shrieked in pain, but still it attacked.

And as he fought, Aaron could not help but return his gaze to a mysterious being he saw floating within one of the digestive sacks. He knew—somehow, *instinctively?*—that this was an angel, but that same something also told him that this was an angel of enormous prestige and power. *An archangel.* Through the opaque skin and milky fluid he could see the ornate armor that hung from the emaciated body of the heavenly being.

"Look upon those that fell before my might, Nephilim," gurgled the monster, assaulting his ears and mind. "He was the Archangel Gabriel—the messenger of God, an extension of the Creator's Word—and he was vanquished as easily as the others."

Aaron's mind was suddenly filled with images of the monster's battle with God's messenger. He saw the winged warrior descend from the heavens, his golden armor glistening beautifully in the dimness of the primordial world. The angel dove beneath the churning waves to confront his quarry, wielding the awesome sword of light.

The battle that Aaron bore witness to could only be described as epic in proportion: a force of the purest light against unfathomable darkness—two opposing powers coming together in a conflict that quite literally rocked the world. The ocean waters around them boiled and churned, kicking up rock, dirt, and silt. Great undersea mountains quaked and crumbled, then the ocean floor split apart, a yawning chasm appearing beneath the opponents, still lost in the midst of conflict. And they tumbled into the gaping abyss, swallowed up by the cataclysmic fury unleashed by their struggle.

The vision came to an abrupt end with the disturbing and final sight of Leviathan engulfing the diminished angel Gabriel within its cavernous mouth. The messenger of God struggled pathetically as he was gradually drawn down the gullet of the beast—immured within one of the behemoth's many stomachs; eternal food for the beast, trapped in a cave, far beneath the sea.

Leviathan laughed within Aaron's mind, a low, gurgling sound, filled with a perverse confidence. *Not even a messenger from God Himself could defeat the monster*, Aaron thought as he continued his battle with the writhing tentacles. *What chance do I have?* he wondered, his efforts against the behemoth beginning to slow. He knew this was what the monster wanted, but he couldn't shake the sense that his struggles against the beast were not going to be enough.

Leviathan's attack was relentless, and it wasn't long before one of the tentacles ensnared the wrist that held his weapon of fire. He tried to pull away, to somehow use the flaming blade against the slimy black limb, but it was to no effect. There was a sudden sharp snap and blinding pain as his wrist was broken. Aaron cried out in shock, watching the sword fall from his grasp, evaporating in the cold, damp air of the cave before it could even touch the ground.

Aaron struggled in the monster's grasp as tentacles wrapped themselves around his arms, his legs, and waist, constricting almost all movement. He found himself lifted from the ground and borne aloft.

Drawn upward to the monster's mouth.

chapter eleven

Leviathan's muscular tendrils hauled him closer. Aaron tried to squirm from their strangling grasp, but the monster's hold upon him was too strong. The sea beast attacked his mind as well, weakening his resolve, taking away his desire to fight back. The spider-things living beneath the behemoth's armored scales chittered and hissed as Aaron's body was drawn steadily upward.

He was almost to Leviathan's mouth, a yawning chasm of razor-sharp teeth, when he heard another voice in his head. It was soft at first, a soothing whisper, like the sound of the wind moving through the trees on a cool fall night. He focused on this new, not unpleasant, tickle and struggled to stay conscious.

He opened his eyes and found himself gazing into one of the many opaque sacks hanging from the gigantic beast—the one that held God's messenger. The Archangel Gabriel's eyes opened, and Aaron knew it was *his* presence within his mind.

"I have long awaited your arrival," whispered a voice that sounded like the most beautiful of stringed instruments.

The voice of the monster was suddenly silenced, drowned out by the enlivening sounds of a cosmic symphony—and despite his dire predicament, Aaron reached out to communicate with this latest entity in his teeming mind.

"How is that possible?" Aaron asked. *"How could you know that I would be here—that I would come?"*

Aaron could sense Leviathan's growing annoyance. Something was blocking its access into his mind, and the monster did not care for that in the least.

"I knew that my torment would not last an eternity," said the angel Gabriel, the celestial music inside his head building to a near deafening crescendo. *"That my successor would eventually come and complete the task assigned to me,"* the angel's voice crooned.

Aaron didn't completely grasp the meaning of the Archangel's words. *"Successor?"* he questioned. *"I don't understand."*

The angel's eyes again began to close. *"There is no time for misunderstanding,"* the angelic being whispered, the sound of his voice growing steadily weaker. *"You are as I was,"* he said. *"A messenger of God."*

"Wait!" Aaron screamed aloud as he was dragged away from the digestive sacks and up toward the monster's face. He squirmed in the tentacles' clutches, the broken bones in his wrist grinding together painfully as he tried again to establish contact with the Archangel. "What do you mean?" he shouted. "I still don't understand!"

A tentacle, its thickness that of a tree trunk, reached down from above the struggling youth and snatched him away from the lesser appendages, drawing him upward.

Aaron found himself hanging upside down by the leg in front of Leviathan's monstrous countenance. The bulging eyes on either side of its head studied him with great interest; its enormous circular mouth puckered and spat as it spoke. "What is there to understand?" asked the horrific sea deity, its voice like the last gasp of a drowning man echoing inside his head. "Your struggles are futile. Surrender to my supremacy and know that it was your life essence, and those of your companions, that finally enabled me to procure my freedom."

Somehow, Leviathan had not heard the angel Gabriel's words. The monster did not hear the angelic warrior proclaim him as a messenger of God, and Aaron began to wonder if it all wasn't some kind of perverse trick on the part of the sea beast—to give him the slightest glimmer of hope and rip it savagely away.

He was brought closer to the gaping hole of a mouth, and Aaron saw himself pathetically reflected in the glassy surface of its bulbous, fishlike eyes, dangling upside down, waiting to be dropped into the cavernous mouth of the ancient, undersea behemoth. *Messenger of God my ass, I don't have a chance in hell*, Aaron thought as he prepared to be consumed.

"That is what it wants you to believe," said the barely audible voice of the Archangel Gabriel. *"That is how it has defeated us all, by making us believe that which is not true."*

Aaron squirmed, the angel's words chasing away the monster's infusion of self-doubt.

"When will you realize the futility of your actions?" Leviathan asked, giving him a violent shake. "Why do you fight when you cannot win, little Nephilim? The time for struggle is past. Now it is time to surrender."

Aaron found the words streaming from his mouth before even realizing what he was going to say.

"I will not surrender to you," Aaron said, a powerful anger building up inside him. He began to thrash, attempting to free himself from the ancient beast.

Leviathan laughed, tightening its grip upon his leg and lowering him toward its yawning mouth. "Courage even in the face of the inevitable," it gurgled. "Perhaps it shall make your life stuff all the more sweet."

The stink that wafted up from the monster's gullet was enough to render a body unconscious, and Aaron tried desperately to hold his breath. The flesh of the sea monster's tentacle was slimy beneath his clawing fingers, and he could not get a good enough grip upon the skin to render any damage. He felt the appendage's hold upon him loosen, and prepared for the fall into oblivion—when the angel Gabriel spoke again.

"I give again to you, my weapon of choice. Take it now as you took it the first time you struggled within the grasp of nightmare. I give to you Bringer of Light—use it well, messenger of God."

Aaron felt the blade of the messenger, Bringer of Light, appear in his hand, and the sharp, grinding pain from his broken wrist immediately eased as the bones miraculously knitted themselves back together.

"What is this?" Leviathan growled, its enormous eyes attempting to focus on him and the weapon that sprang to brilliant life in his grasp.

Aaron felt invigorated. The shroud of despair that had held him in its grasp dissipated like the morning fog in the presence of the rising sun. He swung his body out and swiped his blade across one of the fishlike eyes that ogled him. Bringer of Light cut across the wet surface of the bulging orb, slicing open the gelatinous organ. Leviathan screamed in a mixture of agony and rage—and Aaron was released from its hold.

The monster continued to shriek in pain, its

gigantic mass thrashing in the close quarters of the undersea cave. Aaron landed precariously atop the cluster of sacks hanging from the front of the raging Leviathan. He tried to grab hold, to keep from being thrown from the swaying stomachs. His body slid across the rubbery surface of the digestive organs, sounding much like it did when rubbing a hand upon an inflated balloon. Aaron sunk his fingernails into the fleshy surface and held on.

The sea monster was bucking, bellowing its rage throughout its cave domain, its injured eye swollen closed, weeping streams of thick yellow fluid that resembled egg yoke.

"You shall suffer for that, Nephilim!" it screamed as it bent its body in an attempt to locate him with its remaining sensory organ. "I shall make your internment within my hungry stomach last an eternity. You shall be my favorite meal, and I will savor the taste of you for a very long time!"

Aaron began to slip, his purchase upon the tumorous sacks insecure. His face pressed against the surface of one of the opaque membranes, and he again found himself peering into the wan face of the Archangel Gabriel, floating within the digestive fluids of the behemoth.

"*Messenger*," a voice probed weakly within his brain, "*free me.*" And the angel opened his eyes, their intensity inspiring him to act.

Aaron pulled back his arm with a yell and

brought it forward, hacking at where the digestive sacks connected to Leviathan's chest. The heavenly blade passed through the connective tissue with ease, and the dangling organs fell from the monster's body like ripened fruit from the tree.

Leviathan continued to bellow, throwing its body against its stone prison, causing parts of walls and ceiling to crumble, raining rubble down onto the cave floor.

Aaron let himself fall. He had done his best, cutting away as many of the stomach prisons as possible, but there were just too many and he could not reach them all. Landing atop a pile of the fleshy sacks, he began to cut into the fluid-filled organs, attempting to free those trapped within before the beast overcame its fury.

Thick, milky liquids drained from opened casings, coating the ground in a layer of foul-smelling digestive juices. Leviathan moaned woefully, its great, serpentine mass leaning against the undersea cave's wall, seemingly thrown into a kind of shock—*perhaps as a result of being cut off from its food source*, Aaron guessed wildly, but he knew deep down that the beast would not remain docile for long. It was only a matter of time before its anger would fuel it to strike back at the one who hurt it so.

"You have hurt the beast," a voice said from behind him. Aaron turned to see the emaciated form of the angel Gabriel. His once glorious armor was now the color of a dirty penny, hanging large upon his dripping, skeletal frame. The Archangel swayed, barely conscious, in a puddle of viscous fluid. "Now you must finish the task we failed to complete." He gestured with a skeletal hand to the other sacks, and those still lying within. Bracelets that were probably once worn tight upon thick, muscular wrists jangled loosely, threatening to slip off. "In the name of the Creator, slay the beast Leviathan."

Aaron came toward him. "I . . . I can't do that," he said. He offered Gabriel the sword. "Here," he said. "You do it."

The angel fell to his knees upon the fluid-saturated ground. "That is not possible," Gabriel wheezed. "To do battle with the monster would only quicken my inevitable demise."

Aaron returned to the digestive sacks. "Maybe one of the others could help you," he suggested, fitfully gazing down at the still forms of the other angelic beings that had been held captive in the bellies of the fearsome monster. Many had curled into the fetal position, trapped within a world of Leviathan's making.

"Most are in as dire condition as I am," Gabriel wheezed in response.

Aaron knelt down beside two sacks, which contained his dog and Camael. "Will they be all right?" he asked, laying a trembling hand upon the Labrador's side, feeling for a heartbeat or any sign of life.

"They have not been prisoners of the beast for

long," the Archangel said. "They will survive—if Leviathan does not reclaim them."

The monster stirred, a low, tremulous moan echoing throughout the underwater cavern.

Aaron stood, Bringer of Light still clutched tightly in his hand. "Do you have any idea what you're asking me to do—you want *me to* kill *that?*"

Gabriel tilted his head to one side. "Do you have any idea the extent of power within you?" the angel retorted.

"Nephilim!" the monster raged, its muscular body stretching as high as the ceiling would allow, its injured eye swollen closed and dripping. Its head moved from left to right as it searched for its prey. "I will find you—and all that you are shall belong to *me!*"

Aaron stood rooted, watching as the enormous, sluglike monstrosity began to undulate in his general direction, its tentacles writhing in the air, as if somehow replacing the sensory organ that had been violently stolen away.

"Even the monster knows what resides within you," the angel Gabriel said. "And still you deny it."

Leviathan shambled closer, its tentacles lashing out, snatching at the air as it attempted to find its quarry. "Where are you, Nephilim?" it spat.

"The power I had inside me . . . I think it's gone," Aaron stammered, eyes upon the sea beast. "I've tried to communicate with it, but it doesn't answer. I think Leviathan might have done something and—"

"Is that what you wish happened?" the Archangel asked. "Or is that what actually occurred?"

At first, Aaron didn't understand what the angel was suggesting, but the meaning was suddenly clear.

"I've been inside your mind, Nephilim," Gabriel said, touching the side of his own head with a long, delicate index finger. "I've seen the fear that fills your thoughts."

"I . . . I don't think I'm strong enough to control it," Aaron said flatly, watching with terror-filled eyes as Leviathan drew closer.

"And if it were gone," suggested Gabriel, "you would no longer have to be afraid."

Aaron nodded, ashamed of his fear and that it would allow him to put the lives of his loved ones—as well as the fate of humanity—at risk.

"The power of Heaven is your legacy," the angel explained weakly. "It is this might that exists within you that will allow you to perform your sacred duties as messenger." Gabriel again climbed unsteadily to his feet. "It belongs to you—you are its master."

And Aaron came to the realization that his angelic power had not gone away, but had been there all along, hidden beneath the shroud of his uncertainty—waiting patiently to be unleashed.

"Own this power," the angel said, turning his attention from the boy to the quickly approaching foe. "Show that you are an emissary of Heaven."

Leviathan was almost upon them, and Aaron closed his eyes and looked upon what he had created to keep the power at bay. He imagined standing before a gigantic gate of his own construction, made from the logs of some mighty tree. It was like something he'd seen in the movies used to keep King Kong on his side of Skull Island. Within the face of the gate was a lock, and in the center of the lock, a keyhole. He produced an old-fashioned skeleton key and tentatively brought it toward the keyhole. The gate rattled and shook, as if something of enormous size were waiting on the other side, eager to be set free. He could hear it breathing; slow, steady breaths like a locomotive gradually building to speed.

Tentatively he brought the key to the lock. He knew that this was what had to be done—he could no longer be afraid of the force that shared his body; there was too much at stake for fear. With a deep breath, Aaron turned the key and listened to the sound of the lock as it came undone with a tumbling *clack.*

The slow and steady breathing on the other side of the gate came to an abrupt stop. He could feel its anticipation grow as it suspected what he was about to do. Without further hesitation, Aaron threw open the great wooden gates and set his power free.

Aaron gasped as the archaic markings began to appear upon his flesh. They burned from the inside out, rising to the surface to erupt smoldering and black on the skin of his body. He had no idea what the strange sigils were for, or what they meant, but they were the first sign that the ancient inner power residing within him was about to be unleashed.

The sensation was far less painful this time, and not entirely unpleasant. *It's like the world's biggest head-rush,* he thought as he was caught up in the transformation of his body. Muscles that he'd only recently become aware of contracted spasmodically, pushing the latent wings furled beneath the flesh of his back toward the surface. Aaron winced as the skin split and tore, the feathered appendages that would allow him flight emerging. He flexed the sinewy cluster beneath the skin of his back and felt the strength within the mighty wings as they began to flap.

The power was intoxicating, and Aaron felt himself caught up in the enormity of its strength. It wanted nothing more than to explode out into the world, to vanquish the enemy before it—and then to move on to the next. It was a power of battle that had become part of him, and it reveled in the art of war.

The transformation nearly complete, Aaron gazed with new eyes upon the weapon still clutched within his hand. "This isn't mine," he said, his voice like the purr of a jungle predator. He tossed the blade of light to its originator, the Archangel Gabriel—who caught the sword with ease, taking strength from contact with the radiant weapon.

A sword of Aaron's own design came to life in his hand, and he gazed at the weapon with a growing sense of anticipation. "*This* belongs to me," he said, admiring the blade's potential as it sparked and licked hungrily at the air.

"Yes," Gabriel said with a nod. "I believe it does."

The power sang within him, and Aaron found it hard to remember what exactly he had been so afraid of—but only for the briefest of instants, for the monster Leviathan attacked.

"I've found you, Nephilim," it growled, its ruptured eye still dripping thick streams of yellow fluid, the other wide and bulging. "And what I see, can be made mine."

Before he could act, Aaron felt his mind viciously assaulted, and his perceptions of the here and now suddenly, dramatically altered. He was no longer standing in an underwater cave, sword of fire in hand, a monster of legend looming above him; Aaron now stood in the middle of the playroom of his loving home in Lynn, Massachusetts, his foster parents familiarly nestled into their appropriate pieces of furniture. It was Friday night—movie night at the Stanley household.

"Are you going to sit down and watch the flick, or are you going out?" Tom Stanley asked from his recliner, the plastic box for the video rental in his lap.

Aaron smiled sadly at his foster dad, a mixture of happiness and sorrow washing over him—and he didn't quite remember why he would feel that way.

A new feeling forced its way to the surface of his soul, violently attempting to tear the heartfelt emotions away. Aaron actually twitched, eyes blinking severely, the level of feelings washing over him so intense. *What's going on?* he wondered, too old to blame it all on puberty.

"It's the new Schwarzenegger," his dad said, holding up the plastic case. "The one where his family is killed by terrorists and he gets revenge." There was an excited grin upon his face.

"He always liked those kinds of movies . . . ," said a voice inside his head that sounded more like an animal's growl than his own. And again he shuddered.

"Are you all right, hon?" the only mother he had ever known asked from the corner of the couch. She put down her latest in a long succession of romance novels. "You look a little out of it," she said with genuine concern. "Why don't you sit down, watch the movie, and I'll make you up some soup."

The growling voice inside his head was back. *"That was her first line of defense against all kinds of illness,"* it said, letting the meaning of its statement begin to permeate. *"It didn't help her a bit against Verchiel."*

An anger fueled by sorrow ignited in his

chest, and the palm of his right hand began to grow unusually hot, tingling as if asleep.

Lori Stanley got up. "Go on," she said, touching his shoulders. "Sit with Stevie and Gabriel and I'll make you something to eat." She headed for the kitchen.

For the first time, Aaron noticed his foster brother sitting on the carpet surrounded by blocks of all sizes and shapes. The dog was sleeping soundly beside him, his breathing rhythmic and peaceful. Aaron scratched at the tingling sensation in the palm of his hand and wondered where he had heard the name Verchiel before.

"I really think this is going to be a good one," his dad said excitedly from his recliner, staring at the picture on the front of the video box. Distracted, Aaron gazed down to see that the little boy was spelling something out in the letter blocks upon the carpet. But that was impossible; he knew Stevie could barely talk, never mind spell.

Aaron knelt down beside the child, his body torn by a maelstrom of emotions that were attempting to take possession of him. He hadn't a clue as to what was wrong with him—until he read what Stevie had spelled out upon the floor.

Your mother and father are dead, it said in multi-colored plastic letters, which he unnecessarily remembered had magnets on the back of them so that they could be stuck to the refrigerator.

Aaron sprang to his feet, and a fire sparked

in the center of his hand as his mother returned to the room with a steaming bowl of soup. Aaron was holding a sword of fire now, and he gazed in awe upon it as if he had never seen its like before.

"Sit down, Aaron," his dad said as he motioned with his hand for him to get out of the way of the television. "This is going to be the best movie night ever." Again, Tom motioned for him to sit, to forget all the conflicting emotions running rampant through him—to forget that he was now holding a flaming sword.

"Here's your soup," Lori said, holding the bowl out to him. "It's chicken with stars," she said.

This was what he wanted, more than anything, but something inside him—something very angry and quite powerful—told him that it wasn't to be, that it was all a lie.

He again looked down at the words spelled out in plastic letters.

Your mother and father are dead. The words were like the powerful blows of a sledgehammer, breaking away the false facade of a world that no longer existed, and Aaron began to scream.

He lashed out with his sword of fire, giving in to the rage that tried so hard to show him the deceit of it all. Aaron felt nothing as the weapon of fire passed through the form of his mother. She wailed like the mournful screech of breaks on a rain-soaked highway. His father cried out as well, still eagerly holding on to the video box as his body slumped to one side, consumed by fire.

"It's all a lie," Aaron bellowed, letting the living flame from his weapon extend into the playroom, burning away the untruth—and the screams of the unreal grew all the louder.

Aaron became conscious in the grip of Leviathan, the monster recoiling from the ferocity and violence of his thoughts. This was the personal heaven of his angelic nature unfolding within his skull that the sea beast now bore witness to. A heaven consisting of untruths burned away to reveal reality, the enemy vanquished—consumed in the fires of battle. It was a version of Paradise that Aaron doubted the great beast had ever created in the minds of its prey—a perfect bliss that involved its very own demise.

And it could not stand the thought of it.

The monster howled its displeasure and hurled him away. He could not react fast enough, his wings crimped from being entwined in the multiple tentacles of the beast, and bounced off the cave wall, falling to the rocky floor.

"What's the matter?" Aaron asked as he struggled to his feet and slid across the loose rock. He flexed his ebony wings, their prodigious span fanning the stale air of the undersea cave. "See something you didn't like?"

He sensed that the power within him had a streak of cruelty; exploiting the weaknesses of his enemy, prying away at the chinks in its armor, and that it would stop at nothing to achieve its victory. Aaron wondered exactly how far it would go—and, if it became necessary, was he strong enough to stop it? He would just have to hope that he was.

Aaron spread his wings and sprang into the air, sword at the ready. A savage war cry escaped his mouth that both frightened and excited him with its ferocity. He flew at the swaying monster, ready to bury the flaming weapon into the creature's flesh and end the nightmare's threat to the town of Blithe—as well as to the world.

He slashed at the half-blind beast, his sword of fire connecting repeatedly with the body of Leviathan. Sparks of flame leaped from the weapon's contact with the monster's scaled flesh, but to little avail. The scales were like armor, protecting the ancient threat against his attack. His angelic nature yowled with displeasure, and he attempted to push aside the overwhelming bloodlust so that he could rethink his course of action, but the ferocity was intoxicating, and he continued with his fevered assault upon the beast.

"Strike all you wish, little Nephilim," it gurgled as sparks of flame danced into the air with each new blow upon its seemingly impenetrable scales. "It matters not to me."

One of Leviathan's multitude of limbs lashed out, wrapping around one of his legs. Before he could bring his blade down to sever the connection, the monster acted, whipping him back against the wall with savage ferocity. His head and upper body struck the side of the cave wall, and he felt himself grow numb from the impact.

"They have all thought themselves superior," the monster continued, slapping him against the opposite side of the cave with equal savagery. "The righteous against the wicked—is there ever any doubt against the outcome?"

Leviathan then threw him upon the ground, and it took all the inner strength that he could muster not to slip away into unconsciousness. The inner angel struggled, but it, too, was fighting not to succumb to the ferocity of the attack.

Aaron heard the gigantic animal shift its mass closer—and then what sounded like the fall of heavy rain. He could not begin to discern the source of the sound until he felt the chitinous limbs of one of Leviathan's spawn scurry across his outstretched hand. Its spidery children were crawling out from beneath their master's scales to pour down upon him. Aaron could feel them moving across his back and legs and was filled with revulsion.

"They never could imagine the strength that I amassed," the behemoth boasted. "Overconfidence has always been their downfall."

Aaron felt it again attempting to intrude upon his mind and he blocked it, temporarily locking it behind the fortified fence that he had mentally erected to keep his newly awakened angelic nature isolated. He needed to think, to come up with a way to vanquish the monster before it had a chance to do the same to him, but time was of the essence.

Aaron picked himself up from the ground, the hissing spidery abominations clinging to his clothing, attempting to reach his mouth where they could crawl inside, making him docile enough so that their progenitor could consume him with the least amount of effort. He would have none of that; tearing them from his body by hand and spreading his wings, beating them furiously.

Leviathan loomed closer and opened its damaged eye to glare at him. The injured orb had begun to heal, but the reminder of his sword's cut across it could still be seen.

"Nowhere for you to run, nowhere for you to hide," cooed the beast. "Others far mightier than you have tried to destroy me—and look what has befallen them."

Aaron's glance shot to the severed digestive sacks. He could see that many still lay within the protective cocoons of oblivion, while others, he believed, were most likely dead, their life forces drained away by the nightmare before him.

Leviathan slithered closer, and Aaron gazed up into the monster's flapping mouth, staring into its soft, pink gullet—and an idea began to coalesce.

His angelic nature had received its second wind, and surged forward eager to continue the struggle. Aaron gritted his teeth with exertion, placing a mental choke chain around the powerful force's neck and drew it to him. The power of Heaven fought, wanting to ignite a sword of fire and again leap into the fray—wanting him to battle against the ancient evil from the primordial depths.

But that was not his plan, even though holding back was probably one of the most difficult things he had ever had to do. Aaron stifled screams of pain as the essence of his angelic nature fought against him to be released.

"Not yet," Aaron whispered through gritted teeth, as the monster shambled closer to where he crouched. The beginnings of a heavenly blade sparked in his grasp, but he wished it away, turning his entire attention to the beast that now lorded over him.

"What shall the game be this time, Nephilim?" Leviathan asked, obviously expecting their conflict to resume.

Aaron shook his head, gazing up into the face of the horrific nightmare that was Leviathan. "No games," he told the beast. He held up his empty hands to the behemoth, showing the monstrosity that they were empty of weapons. "I can't fight you anymore."

Leviathan laughed, a horrible, rumbling gurgle. "How sensible of you, Nephilim," it said, tentacles squirming in the air with anticipation.

Aaron stood beneath the monster and spread his arms in a show of surrender. His body was still racked with pain as he tried to contain the furious forces that fought desperately to emerge and to defend itself; but he held it back, for it was not yet time.

"Take me," he told the wormlike creature that had existed since the dawn of time.

And Leviathan entwined him in its clutches, pulling him up toward its hungry mouth. "I shall use your power well," it said, staring at him with its cold, unblinking eyes, viscous saliva beginning to pour from its circular orifice to run down the length of its black, glistening body.

"Eat me," Aaron shouted. "And I hope you choke!" he added as the muscular appendages shoved him into its gaping maw, and he was swallowed up whole.

The first thing that Aaron noticed was the unbelievable stench. It stank even worse on the inside. He recalled the putrid aroma of a single mouse that had died in the kitchen wall of the Stanley house, and how he had thought nothing could smell as bad.

He couldn't have been more wrong.

He would rather have been wearing the dead rodent around his neck as jewelry for the rest of his life than endure the overwhelming stench of Leviathan's insides.

If it wasn't for the thick lubricating fluids that flowed upon him as the muscular throat of the beast contracted, sending him down toward its stomachs, there was the chance that the aroma of the monster's internal workings could very well have rendered him unconscious.

The excretions of Leviathan's digestive system were beginning to have their effects upon him also. His skin burned, and he felt a wave of undeniable fatigue attempting to purge the fight from his spirit. Even the angelic presence became increasingly docile, and Aaron knew that it would soon be time to put his plan into effect.

The interior of the beast gurgled and spat as it moved his mass through a series of powerful, muscular spasms—down what Aaron believed to be its esophagus—on his way to one of the still remaining digestive sacks hanging from Leviathan's body. It was getting difficult to breathe, and he felt his eyes grow heavy. Aaron wrestled with the idea of taking a bit of a nap before continuing with his course of action, but thought better of it, remembering the fate of the angelic beings that had been food for the great evil.

Perversely enough, the trip down the monster's gullet reminded him of one of those amusement park water slides as he attempted to bend his body in such a way that he could see where he was going. It was black as pitch within the monster's stomach, and Aaron managed to summon a ball of fire and maintain it as he continued his twisting journey to the belly of the beast. Half of him wished he didn't need the source of light, for the insides of a creature of chaos was not the most pleasant of places to see.

There was an abrupt turn in the food tube, and Aaron suddenly found himself about to be deposited within one of the remaining digestive organs. This was not part of his plan, and he summoned a knife of fire, stabbing it into the fleshy wall of the digestive passage, halting his progress. He felt his surroundings roil, and knew he had caused the great beast discomfort. *The son of a bitch doesn't yet know the meaning of the word*, he thought, releasing his hold upon the power within him—and even though more manageable than it had been before he was eaten, it took full advantage of a chance for freedom. If his plan was successful, Leviathan would have much more to worry about than simple discomfort.

An incredible surge of energy coursed through his fluid covered body, and he felt his lethargy immediately burned away. He positioned himself within the stomach passageway and unfurled his wings as far as he possibly could; still holding on to the knife blade that acted as an anchor, preventing him from being pulled further into Leviathan's stomach. Now wielding the full extent of his latent power,

Aaron conjured an awesome sword of heavenly fire, illuminating his nauseating environment—and immediately began to put his plan in motion.

He was about to show Leviathan the disastrous effects of eating something that did not agree with it.

If it were capable, the beast Leviathan would have smiled.

As it swallowed down its latest morsel, a wave of contentment passed through the monster the likes of which it had never experienced. Leviathan could feel the pulse of the Nephilim's power within it, and knew that this source of strength would be what would finally allow it to emerge from its prison of rock, and claim the world above as its own.

It watched the others that had once been part of its nourishment, the angelic creatures, useless husks, drained and sprawled about on the floor of its prison, and realized that none had made it feel as glorious as it did now. The spawn moved excitedly beneath their parent's protective scales, sensing that it would soon be time to leave the cave and emerge out into the world, where its reign would commence.

It imagined that the Creator, in all His infinite wisdom, would send others to smite him—soldiers of the heavenly realm—that would all meet a similar fate as those who had come before. With the Nephilim's strength, there was nothing that could stop Leviathan from recreating the world in his own likeness.

Sated by the mere promise of new angelic energies, Leviathan prepared itself for the transforming influx of power that would soon awash it. It leaned its colossal, wormlike bulk against the cave wall and imagined what was next in its future. After countless millennia, it had the means to be free. The denizen of the depths would send its spawn out of the cave, to the settlements beyond, bringing the inhabitants, now under its control, to Blithe. Now it would have the substantial numbers and tools needed to be liberated from its rocky prison.

And then its work would begin.

The monster fantasized of a world transformed—sculpted as a representation of its own chaotic nature. It saw a place covered with churning seas, most of the landmasses swallowed up by volcanic upheaval, the skies gone black from volumes of ash expelled into the atmosphere to blot out the hated sun. And all the life upon the new world, that teemed upon what was left of the blighted land, and swam beneath the dark, ocean depths, would praise its name in worship.

"Leviathan," it imagined they would proclaim. "How blessed we are that you have touched us with your resplendent glory. Praise be the Lord of the deep, hallowed be thy—"

It felt a sharp twinge of pain in the lower internal regions of its mass, a burning sensation that seemed to be growing. The monster removed itself from the wall where it had reclined, its head scraping the roof of the under-sea cavern as it rose.

"What is this?" it asked in a sibilant whisper full of shock and surprise as the discomfort intensified. "What is happening?"

Never had it experienced such agony; it was as if there was a fire raging within its body—*but how is that possible?* it wondered. The heat of its pain was intensifying, the blistering warmth expanding up from the nether regions of its ser-pentine trunk to spread throughout.

"This cannot be happening," Leviathan exclaimed as the first of the remaining digestive sacks exploded, the fluids contained within brought to a boil from the raging internal tem-peratures of its body. Leviathan moaned in agony, powerless to act. Another of the sacks ruptured, spraying the walls in a bubbling stream—followed by another, and then another.

The monster swooned, its pain-racked form crashing into the rocky surface of the cave walls. The spawn, normally protected beneath its armor of scales, rained down to the cavern floor, scampering about in frenzied panic—driven to madness by the pain of their progenitor.

Leviathan wanted nothing more than to flee its prison, to have an opportunity to show the

Creator that it, too, had a reason to exist. In its fevered thoughts it saw the glimpses of a paradise of its own design fading quickly away. It saw the black, roiling oceans full of life that it had helped reconfigure—a world of chaos that looked upon it as God and Master.

"It would have been magnificent," Leviathan moaned as the sword of fire erupted from the center of its body—and something that burned like a star emerged from the smoldering wound.

chapter twelve

Camael slowly removed himself from the ruptured digestive organ and gazed about his foreign surroundings with a cautious eye.

While trapped within the prison he was made to believe that he had found the angelic paradise that was Aerie—and all the centuries of isolation and conflict he had experienced had come to an end. The prophecy had occurred: The fallen angels of Earth forgiven by Heaven. It was bliss.

As he looked around the subterranean cave, the reality of the situation was driven painfully home. He had not found Aerie, and where he now stood was the farthest from Paradise any angel could possibly be.

A mournful wail rose in intensity, reverberating around the cavern, awakening the angel further to his environment. Camael turned to see the monster Leviathan in what appeared to be the grip of torture. The sea behemoth thrashed, its body viciously pounding off of the cave walls as it shrieked in pain.

A sword of fire grew in his hand, a caution in case he should need to defend himself.

"He is accomplishing what we could not," said a voice nearby, and Camael turned to the Archangel Gabriel, withered and wan, leaning back against the stone wall.

Camael bowed his head, recognizing the angel for what and who he was. "Of whom do you speak, great one?" Camael asked, returning his attentions to the flailing beast.

"The Nephilim," the desiccated emissary of Heaven whispered. "The latest messenger of God."

"Aaron," Camael gasped as Leviathan continued its dance of agony. He watched awestruck as the skin of the beast smoldered, the protrusions that dangled obscenely from the monster's front, and of which he had been captive within, exploding, their contents spraying the air with a steaming mist.

"It would have been magnificent," he heard the creature of nightmare rattle as a weapon of fire suddenly tore through its midsection, and a warrior angel—one he first bore witness to only a few weeks ago—stepped from the gash in what seemed a mockery of birth.

He was about to call out to the Nephilim, but something stayed his tongue. Camael observed the half-breed, the offspring of angel and human, and was startled, and perhaps even a little concerned by what he saw.

The Nephilim jumped from the wound in the sea beast's stomach, his black-feathered wings flapping furiously, attempting to dry away the internal fluids that stained their sleek ebony beauty. In his hand he held a sword of fire—a weapon so fierce that it could rival those carried by the elite soldiers of Heaven. This was not the newly born being of angelic power that erupted to life mere weeks ago to avenge loved ones viciously slain, Camael observed. This was something all together different.

Camael watched as the transformed youth rose into the air before the agonizing beast, his mighty wings beating the air, lifting him to hover before the face of his enemy.

Leviathan lashed out at the Nephilim, its whiplike tentacles attempting capture, but falling upon empty air, the angel's movements were so swift.

"Damn you," Leviathan roared, its thick, green life stuff draining out from the gaping stomach wound to pool upon the cave floor. "Damn you—and the master you serve."

Aaron hovered before the snarling face of the beast, sword poised to strike, and Camael marveled at the sight of it.

"Got a message from the big honcho upstairs," Camael heard the Nephilim cry as he brought the flaming blade down in a powerful arc aimed at Leviathan's head. "You're dead."

The fire blade cleaved through the incredible thickness of the sea beast's skull with a resounding *crack*—the majority of the fearsome weapon buried deep within its monstrous cranium. It thrashed wildly in a futile attempt to dislodge the flaming weapon, but then grew impossibly still.

Aaron withdrew the sword and held it proudly above his head, powerful wings beating, holding him aloft. A fearsome cry of victory filled the air, and Camael stared in awe as the gigantic body of the ancient sea deity began to burn. The first flames shot up from Leviathan's head wound in a geyser of orange fire, the ravenous heat spreading down the length of the monster's enormity—its scaled flesh, muscle, and bone food for the heavenly flames.

Aaron flew down to the cave floor just as the monster's body collapsed in a gigantic pyre of smoldering ash, and strode menacingly toward Camael. The spawns of Leviathan scrambled about the cave floor, their shells aflame—the final remnants of the ancient sea monster left alive—but not for long.

Camael clutched his own weapon, unsure of the Nephilim's true intentions. It would not be the first time that he had borne witness to a half-breed's descent into madness after manifesting the full extent of its heavenly might.

Aaron stood before him, heavenly armament in hand, and he studied the fearsome countenance of the Nephilim. In his weakened state, Camael wasn't sure if he could survive a battle with such an adversary, but prepared himself nonetheless. Neither spoke, but the angel warrior watched for the slightest hint of attack. If there was to be a battle, his first strikes would need to be lethal.

"That thing really pissed me off," Aaron said as a small smile played across his warrior's features. "Glad to see you're all right."

And Camael lowered his sword, confident that the Nephilim's mental state was still intact—at least for the moment.

Aaron placed his hand on Gabriel's side, watching the rise and fall of the dog's breathing. The Labrador's yellow coat was saturated with slime. "Hey," he said softly, giving his best friend a gentle shake. "It's time to get up."

At first, the animal did not respond, his mind still in the embrace of doggy paradise. Aaron shook him again a bit harder. "Gabriel, wake up."

"I am awake," replied the archangel wearily, still resting his emaciated frame against the cave wall.

Aaron looked up. "I was talking to the dog," he told the messenger of God. "His name is Gabriel, too." He smiled briefly and looked back at his friend, who was finally beginning to stir. "Hey, pally, you awake yet?"

The dog stretched his four limbs and neck, emitting a low, throaty groan that began somewhere in the lower regions of his broad chest. Then he sighed, his dark brown eyes coming open. *"I was having a dream, Aaron,"* he said sleepily. *"I was chasing rabbits and having lots of good things to eat."*

Aaron stroked the dog's head lovingly. "You can do all that stuff out here—without being eaten by a sea monster."

The dog lifted his head and gazed about. *"Where are we?"* he asked, sitting up. *"The last thing I remember . . . the old woman,"* he said, a wide-eyed expression of shock on his canine face. *"She spit something at me, and it made me numb."*

"Yep, I know," Aaron nodded. "But I think we've taken care of that," he said, and looked in the direction of the still smoldering remains of the mythological sea monster.

"The spawn cannot continue to exist without the beast's mind," Camael said, standing over the fleshy sacks that Aaron had liberated from the monster's body. He was checking to see which of the captives of Leviathan were still living. "They were all part of one great beast—and the parts cannot survive without the whole."

Gabriel stiffly climbed to his feet and shook, spattering the surrounding area with the digestive juices that still clung to his fur.

"Watch that," Aaron said, covering his face, his wings reflexively coming around to block the spray. "I've got enough of that crap covering me."

"Then you won't notice a little more," the dog said, and smiled that special smile unique to the Labrador.

"Maybe there's still a chance I can shove you back into one of those stomachs," Aaron grumbled with mock seriousness, giving the dog a squinty-eyed stare. Gabriel barked and wagged his tail, none the worse for his experience being captive in the gut of a sea beast.

"Who's he?" the dog suddenly asked, coming forward, his nose twitching.

Aaron noticed the angel Gabriel now stood by him, and seemed to be studying his dog of the same name.

"Gabriel," Aaron said to the animal, "this is Gabriel." He motioned toward the archangel.

Gabriel padded closer, nose still sniffing, tail wagging cautiously. *"That's a very handsome name,"* the dog told the angelic being.

The archangel looked from the dog to Aaron, a quizzical expression on his gaunt features. "You named this animal—after *me?"*

Aaron shrugged his shoulders. "Not specifically. It's just a very regal-sounding name. When he was a pup he looked like a Gabriel to me, that's all."

"I was quite adorable when I was a puppy," the dog said with a tilt of his blocky head.

The still weakened angel carefully walked toward the dog, reaching out a trembling hand to touch the animal's head. The Lab seemed to have no problem with that, licking the angel's hand affectionately.

"This animal has been changed," the archangel said, stroking the fur on the side of Gabriel's handsome face. "It is not as it should be." The angel looked back, as if seeking an explanation.

"Gabriel is very important to me," Aaron began. "He was hurt—near death. I saved him."

"You saved him," the angel repeated, holding the dog's face beneath the chin and gazing into his dark chocolate eyes. "And so much more."

"*He did*," Gabriel said, looking back.

"What other wonders can you perform, Aaron Corbet of the Nephilim?" the angel Gabriel asked, fascination in his tone.

Aaron didn't know what to say, feeling self-conscious beneath the scrutinizing eyes of the messenger of God. "I really don't know, but . . ."

"He is the chosen of the prophecy," Camael spoke up. The former leader of the Powers was kneeling beside the now deflated digestive sacks, and the remains of the angelic beings they contained. He gazed at the bodies of the heavenly creatures, many just barely alive—on the verge of death. "What other wonders is he capable of?" Camael asked sadly among the desiccated and the dying. "He can send our fallen brethren home."

Aaron remembered what he had done for the dying Ezekiel—how his newly awakened power had forgiven the fallen angel of his sins and allowed his return to Heaven. This ability, this power of redemption, was what the ancient prophecy that had taken over his life was supposedly all about, and whether he liked it or not, it was his job to reunite the fallen angels of Earth with their Creator.

He found himself drawn to the dying angels, his entire body beginning to tingle as if some great electrical charge were building in strength inside him. Aaron was becoming familiar with these feelings. He moved amongst the withered bodies, their life forces taken by the voracious appetites of a creature of chaos, and felt an incredible sadness overtake him. *How long—how many centuries has the monster been drawing them here?* he wondered gazing down at what were once things of awesome beauty—now nothing more than empty shells of their former glory. Those that had fallen from grace, soldiers in service to the Creator, twisted mockeries of angelic life created for servitude: They were all here, lying amongst one another, all desperately in need of one thing that he was capable of bestowing upon them.

Release.

Aaron felt their great sadness—their disgrace, as the churning supernatural power inside him settled in a seething ball at the center of his chest. He knew precisely what to do; it now felt like second nature to him—like breathing, or blinking his eyes.

He laid his hands upon them, one after another—the vortex of power swirling at his center coursing down the length of his arms into his hands. Whether they be Orisha, fallen, or heavenly elite, Aaron touched them all, igniting their dying essences with the force of redemption. "It's over now," he said to them, their bodies glowing like stars, fallen from the night skies to show the fabulous extent of their beauty.

Camael stepped back, bathed in the radiance of their transformation, and Aaron wondered if it was only awe that he saw expressed upon the angel warrior's face, or was it envy?

What the angels had become, as sustenance for a monster's hunger, was no longer a concern—burned away to expose the final flames of divine brilliance that still thrived in each of them.

"You're free," Aaron said as they hovered above the cave floor, reveling in the experience of their rebirth. He spread his wings of shining black and opened his arms. "Time to go home," he proclaimed, and with those words spoken, the dank, eerie darkness of Leviathan's lair was filled with the light of the divine, and any trace of evil still alive within the monster's dwelling was routed out and annihilated in purging rays of heavenly brilliance.

The vivified angels gravitated toward the

Archangel Gabriel, orbiting around the messenger of God, bathing him in their luminous auras—and through the light, Aaron could see that Gabriel was growing stronger, gaining sustenance from his angelic brothers.

Aaron felt at peace as he watched the long-suffering creatures of Heaven reunite, and let his angelic countenance recede back into his body—sated, for now. The arcane sigils that were etched upon his skin started to fade, and his wings furled, gradually withdrawing beneath the flesh and muscle of his back. Both Camael and his dog had joined him, not wanting to interfere in any way with the once-imprisoned angels' communion.

"They're very happy to see one another again," the dog said, tail wagging happily.

"They have been too long without the company of their own kind," Camael said, his eyes riveted to the scene before him, and Aaron questioned if the warrior was not in some way speaking for himself as well.

The Archangel Gabriel was restored to his true glory, armor glistening as if freshly forged and polished, wings the color of a virgin snowfall opening from his back. The wingspan of the messenger was enormous, and he curled them around the children of Heaven, drawing them closer to him.

"We have much to thank you for, fellow messenger," the archangel said in a rich, powerful voice that vibrated in the air like the lower notes played on a church organ. "The monster has been vanquished—and our freedom regained."

Aaron was speechless; even after all that he had seen over the past life-changing weeks, the sight before him filled him with awe. They all floated in the air now, Gabriel as the center of their universe, all those who had survived their ordeal, enwrapped in his loving embrace. He was taking them back—the Archangel Gabriel was escorting them home.

"Know that my blessing goes with you on your perilous journey, brave Nephilim," the angel continued, "and that your acts of heroism shall be spoken of in the kingdom of God."

His dog nudged his hand with his head. *"Did you hear that, Aaron?"* he asked excitedly. *"They're going to be talking about you in God's kingdom."*

Aaron petted his ecstatic friend, still mesmerized by the awesome vision before him.

"With these acts, you have done much to expunge the sins of the father and to fulfill the edicts of prophecy—"

Aaron was so caught up in the melodious sounds of the angel's proclamation of thanks that he didn't immediately catch the meaning of the last sentence—but it gradually sank in, permeated his brain, and alarm bells began to sound.

He hadn't even heard the final words of gratitude spoken by the messenger. The Archangel Gabriel had lifted his head toward the ceiling of the cave, the heavenly glow about them all growing in intensity. Bringer of Light had appeared in his hand, and he pointed the mighty blade toward the cave roof—toward their celestial destination beyond the ceiling of rock and the world of man above.

Aaron charged forward, shielding his eyes from the blinding light of their ascension. "Wait," he cried as he tried to find the Archangel within the radiant spectacle. "Did you say the sins of the father?"

He could just about make out the outline of the angel messenger at the center of the expanding ball of light. Through squinted eyes he saw that Gabriel was looking at him. "My father's sins?" Aaron asked, wanting desperately for the emissary of Heaven to clarify what he had said. "Do you know who my father was? Please . . ."

The light burned so brightly now that he had no choice but to turn away, or go blind.

"You are your father's son," Gabriel said within the light of Heaven. "At first I did not see it, but then it was oh so obvious."

His back to the departing creatures now seemingly composed of living light, Aaron begged for answers from the messenger. "If you know who he is, can't you tell me something—anything . . . please!"

Aaron could feel the pull of the celestial powers as the angels were drawn up to Heaven. He wanted nothing more than to turn around and throw himself into the light, to prevent

Gabriel from returning to God's kingdom—until the Archangel told him what he knew.

There were sounds like the world's largest orchestra tuning their instruments all at the same time—and he knew that it was only a matter of seconds before Gabriel and the others were gone from this plain of existence, taking their valuable knowledge with them.

Aaron fell to his knees upon the cave floor, both physically and emotionally drained.

"You're the messenger," he said, holding out all hope that he would be heard. "Give me a message . . . give me something."

There was a sudden flash of brilliance—and the cavern was filled with an eerie silence as the denizens of Heaven returned to their homes, but not before he heard the whispering voice of the Archangel Gabriel in his ear. "You have your father's eyes."

chapter thirteen

The people of Blithe were vomiting—and Aaron imagined he knew exactly how they must feel. No, he didn't have some crablike creature living inside his chest, but he had just received the very first pieces of information he had ever learned about his *real* father; that the prophecy had something to do with his father's sins, and that he had his father's eyes. He thought he might be sick.

Aaron, Camael, and Gabriel moved through the winding passage that led up from Leviathan's lair to one of the many chambers that had been excavated out of the rock by the townspeople under the sea monster's thrall.

"*Gross,*" Gabriel said, and Aaron couldn't have agreed more. The people, who up until Leviathan's demise had been busily clearing away tons of rock and dirt in an attempt to free the beast, had stopped their work. They had dropped their tools and were bent over in obvious pain—their bodies racked with vomiting and throwing up the horrible things that had crawled inside to control their actions.

"Are they all right?" Aaron asked, wrinkling his nose in disgust at the repellant sounds of people in the midst of being sick.

"Their bodies are rejecting Leviathan's invasive spawn," the angel warrior said, rather blasé. "I would imagine they will be fine—as soon as the dead creatures and their nests are expelled from the body."

The floor of the smaller chamber was puddled with all manner of foulness, and the already decaying remains of the spiderlike things that had taken up residence in their bodies.

Aaron wasn't exactly sure how he felt about what he had learned; it wasn't as if he had been given a phone number or a home address. The identity of the man—*angel*—that had sired him was still a complete mystery, and one that he really couldn't afford to think about right now. He decided that he would deal with it later, when things had calmed down—when things were back to normal. He laughed to himself, as if his life could ever be that way again.

"I wonder how long those things have been inside them?" Aaron asked to distract himself as they proceeded from the smaller cavern, his level of disgust quickly on the rise.

"Most likely since Verchiel wholeheartedly abandoned his holy mission and became obsessed with preventing the prophecy from becoming a reality," Camael said as they walked a tunnel that would, he hoped, take them to the surface.

"So this is something else I can be blamed for?" Aaron asked, feeling the dirt pathway of the tunnel beneath his feet begin to slant upward. They continued to pass the people of Blithe, many of them passed out from the exertion of purging the foreign invaders from their bodies.

"In a way, yes," the angel said. "By ignoring their tasks, the Powers have allowed the forces of chaos to take root in the world, growing in strength, unabated. I shudder to think of what other malignant purveyors of wickedness are hiding in the shadows of the world."

"Great," Aaron responded with a heavy sigh. "Wouldn't want to be let off easy or anything. I wonder if I have anything to do with global warming?" he asked, his words dripping sarcasm. "We might want to look into that."

Gabriel ran up ahead of them and had begun to bark excitedly. *"We're almost to the surface,"* he cried, waiting until they caught up, and then running up ahead. The dog was as sick of being underground as they were, Aaron imagined, and wanted nothing more than to breathe in some nice fresh air.

They emerged from the tunnel out into the

main excavation in the heart of the former boat factory. Aaron noticed that the heavy digging machinery had been silenced, and the only sound that could be heard throughout the air of the place was that of retching. Everywhere he looked, somebody was being sick or incapacitated as a result of being sick.

"This is just too much," Aaron said, taking it all in. "Those things must have been living inside just about everybody in town."

An angled road of dirt had been constructed on the floor of the dig so that trucks and such could be driven down into the hole, and Aaron and his companions used the packed-earth path to ascend to the lip of the excavation at ground level.

As the three moved toward the door that would take them out of the factory, and walked around the violently ill, being careful to step over the reeking puddles that contained the decomposing corpses of Leviathan's children, Aaron caught sight of Katie McGovern and went to her. "Katie," he said as he approached. "Are you all right?" His guess about the filthy man in the cave veterinary clinic had been correct, for her former boyfriend Kevin was with her, and they both gazed at him slack-jawed, their bodies racked with chills. Aaron saw no recognition in Katie's eyes, and he began to feel afraid.

"What's the matter with them?" he asked Camael, who now stood by his side staring at the two as he was.

"Shock, I'd imagine," the angel said. "Their minds are attempting to adjust to the horrors they have experienced. The human mind is a wondrous invention indeed," he said as he stepped closer to Katie's former fiancé. Camael reached out and grabbed the man by the chin, looking deeply into his eyes. "By the morrow they'll have only the vaguest idea that something had happened to them at all," he said, as if attempting to get a glimpse of the inner workings of a human being. "To most, it will become the distant memory of a horrible nightmare." He let Kevin's face go and proceeded to the door. "Such is the coping mechanism of the mortal brain."

Aaron and Gabriel followed the angel out into the early morning dawn. Outside the door, Chief Dexter leaned against his patrol car. He had thrown up onto the windshield, and it looked as though he wasn't quite finished yet. Aaron quickly looked away. "So they won't remember any of this?" he asked the angel who was now striding toward the parking lot.

Gabriel sniffed around the tires of the parked cars, completely disinterested in their conversation. There was valuable sniffing time to be recouped.

"They'll remember, but their minds will shape the event into something that they will be able to accept—no matter how odd or unlikely," Camael answered. "It's how their minds work—how they were designed. And those that do remember the reality of the situation, and dare to speak of it, will be ostracized and labeled as insane."

"Nice," Aaron said, a little taken aback by the angel's cold interpretation of the human psyche. He was silent for the moment, digesting the angelic warrior's words, and decided that he didn't buy it. "If that's how our poor human brains work, then how come I didn't chalk up all this angel crap to eating bad tuna or a high fever due to some rare African virus?"

The angel stopped and turned to stare. "You are Nephilim," Camael said, as if that would be more than enough of an answer.

"Yeah, but I'm still human, right?" Aaron said, staring at the angel and gazing into his steely gray eyes.

On the outskirts of the parking lot, he waited for the angel to respond. Camael remained silent—but the lack of an answer spoke volumes.

"What are you trying to say?" Aaron asked nervously.

It was then that the angel spoke. "You were sired by an angel. You are no more human than I am."

It felt as though he'd been struck. Even though deep down inside, Aaron already knew this, hearing it come out of Camael's mouth was like a whack with a two-by-four between the eyes.

I'm not human, he thought, letting the concept rattle around inside his brain. Could his life be any weirder?

He again heard the Archangel Gabriel's final

words to him—before the angel had taken the express bus to Heaven. The words about his father.

"The Archangel Gabriel said that what I was doing—the prophecy?—was somehow connected to the sins of my father," Aaron said to his angel companion as they reached the padlocked gate.

"Yes," Camael said as a sword of flame came to life in his hands and he severed the chain with a single slice. "And he also said that you have his eyes." Camael pushed open the gate and strode through onto the road.

Aaron held back, waiting for his dog to finish sniffing around a patch of weeds.

"Do you know who he is, Camael?" Aaron asked as his dog trotted over to join him. "My father—do you know who my father is?"

The angel had continued to walk up the road, but he stopped and slowly turned. "I do not, no," he said, shaking his head. "But what I do know is that he must have been an angel of formidable power to have sired one like you." Camael then promptly turned away, continuing on his journey.

"*I think he just paid you a compliment, Aaron,*" Gabriel said as he walked alongside him.

Aaron smiled slightly. "I think you might be right there, Gabe."

Berkely Street was deathly quiet in the early morning stillness, as was the rest of Blithe. Aaron removed a pair of sweatpants and shirt from the backseat of his car and prepared to put them on over his filthy and ripped clothing.

"I think I might have an extra sweatshirt," he said to Camael, gazing at the angel's filthy suit with a wrinkled nose.

"That will be unnecessary," he said.

And Aaron watched with amazement as the accumulated dirt and grime on his companion's suit faded away before his eyes, leaving it as if it had just come from the cleaners. The angel then adjusted his tie, glancing casually in his direction.

"Let me guess," Aaron said as he pulled the sweatshirt down over his head. "I could do that, too, if I just applied myself."

Camael was about to respond, but Aaron put up a hand to silence him; he didn't have the time or energy for a dissertation right now. He finished putting on the rest of his clean clothes and checked out his reflection in the side mirror of his car. It would have to do for now. That was all he needed, for Mrs. Provost to see him looking like he'd been through World War III. It was going to be hard enough to explain what had happened and how she had come to be locked in the cellar.

Camael studied the quaint house with squinted eyes. "And you say that the old woman attacked you?"

"Yeah," Aaron said as he combed his unruly hair with his fingers. "I knocked her out and put her in the cellar. I didn't want to take the risk of her letting the other people in town know I was on to them."

"I'm very hungry after being inside the belly of a monster," Gabriel declared, and hurriedly headed up the walk to the front door. *"I wonder if she'll have any meat loaf?"*

"Not if she's been locked in the basement all night, pal," he said, coming up behind the dog and reaching for the doorknob.

It was unlocked, and Aaron swung the door wide—and was immediately hit with the smell of something cooking, something that made his belly ache and come to the realization that Gabriel wasn't the only one who was very hungry.

"Mrs. Provost?" he called out, looking around the foyer and the area around it. Strangely enough, it showed no sign of their struggle. They all moved toward the kitchen, toward the wonderful smell of breakfast cooking, Camael backing up the rear.

"Mrs. Provost?" he said again as he came around the door frame and saw the older woman at the stove. She was wearing an apron and was frying up some bacon. The old woman turned momentarily from her cooking to give him a smile. "Morning," she said, reaching up with a white bandaged hand to brush away a stray whisp of white hair from her forehead. "Knew the smell of cooking would get you in here." She went back to work, carefully favoring the injured hand.

"What happened to your hand?" he asked her, knowing full well that she had burned it on his sword during their scuffle. She was placing some strips of bacon onto a folded paper towel on the stove, and Gabriel went to her, tail wagging. She was careful to finish up what she was doing before petting the animal with her good hand.

"I'm not really sure," she said, rubbing the dog's ears. "Think I took a bit of a spill down the cellar steps last night," she said kind of dreamily, straining to recall what had happened to her. "Must've knocked myself senseless and touched something hot on the furnace."

She peeled some more strips of the breakfast meat out of the package and laid them in the greasy pan. "Even found a way to lock myself inside," she said with a laugh. "Good thing I found a spare skeleton key down there or I'd still be locked up." The old woman was making sure that the bacon was lined up straight in the pan. "Probably should go see the doctor to rule out concussion or anything," she added. Gabriel lay down on the floor at her feet, gazing up at her adoringly.

Aaron turned and looked at Camael behind him. The angel had been precisely right. Mrs. Provost's brain had done exactly as he described. It had attempted to rationalize the bizarreness of the situation, steering clear of anything that would be too difficult to explain or comprehend.

Mrs. Provost placed her fork down and walked to the refrigerator, all the while under the watchful eye of his Labrador. "I was just about to cook up some eggs," she said, pulling on the fridge door to open it. "My father always used to say that a big breakfast could cure what ails you." She removed the carton of fresh white eggs. "Thought today might be a good day to take his advice."

Camael had not willed himself invisible this time, and Aaron caught her staring at the large, older man behind him—too stubborn to ask his identity. She would wait until he got around to explaining who Camael was.

"This is my friend," he said in introduction. "The one who had some business up in Portland?" She nodded slowly, remembering the conversation that they'd had the first night over supper. "He just got back this morning," he explained.

Camael was silent, studying the old woman just as she was studying him.

"Is he staying for breakfast?" she asked, taking the eggs with her to the stove.

Aaron was about to answer for the angel, when Camael suddenly spoke for himself. "I will have French fries," he said, stunning Aaron with his answer.

Mrs. Provost, completely unfazed by the angel's request, reached down to the stove and pulled it open. A new delicious aroma wafted out of the oven with a blast of heat. There was something cooking inside on a metal sheet.

"Don't have any French fries, but how about home fries—will they do?" she asked. "My husband, God rest his soul, used ta tell me that I made the best home fries in New England." She used an oven mitt covered in a pattern of bananas to remove the hot pan of browned, chopped potatoes from the stove.

"If you like French fries, you're going to love these," Aaron told the angel, his mouth beginning to water.

"Then I will have—home fries," he said, eyeing the breakfast dish now resting atop the stove.

It was all pretty strange and quite amazing, Aaron mused as he finished giving Gabriel his breakfast and watched the kindly old woman expertly crack the last of the eggs into the frying pan, making breakfast as if it were just like any other day of the week. It was hard for him to wrap his brain around the concept. Less than two hours ago he had been fighting for his life against a force that could very well have threatened the world—but here he was now, about to sit down to a big breakfast of bacon, eggs, and home fries. The realization that his life had dramatically changed was again driven home with the force of an atomic blast—and with every new day, it seemed to change more and more. Aaron wondered if he'd ever get used to it, if it would ever seem as mundane as sitting down to eat breakfast.

Shaking some salt onto his eggs, he watched the angel Camael take a tentative bite of the home fries and begin to chew. A look that could only be described as pleasure spread across his goateed face, and he greedily began to eat.

Will my life ever seem so mundane again? he wondered, watching as an angel of Heaven consumed a plate of home-fried potatoes beside him.

He seriously doubted it.

Miss you. Love Aaron.

Aaron sat back in the desk chair, contemplating the last words he had typed in his e-mail to Vilma. *Is it too strong?* he wondered, fingers hovering over the keyboard as he tried to decide. His feelings for the girl back home hadn't even come close to changing, and the more he thought about her, the longer he spent away from her—the stronger they seemed to become.

An all too familiar sadness washed over him as he wondered if he would ever see the pretty Brazilian girl again. He knew it was for her own good that he stay away—Verchiel would certainly think nothing of using her to get to him—but a selfish part of him wanted to be with her, no matter the consequences.

Aaron read through the e-mail again, smirking at how boring it all sounded—if only he could write even a portion of what he'd been experiencing.

Miss you. Love Aaron.

He wondered what Vilma was doing just then. It was early Sunday morning, and he guessed that she probably wasn't even up yet. He wouldn't have been, either, but they had to get going and continue his search for Stevie. He always loved sleeping late on Sundays, reading the *Globe* with a big glass of milk and a couple of Dunkin' Donuts that his foster dad would buy. But that was then.

Aaron read the e-mail one last time and deemed it perfectly fine. *What do I have to lose?* He clicked on the Send button and watched his letter disappear into the electronic ether. *No turning back now,* he thought, in more ways than one. There was only the road ahead of him now, and at the end of that road he hoped to find his little brother, and maybe a chance at a normal life—if fulfilling an ancient prophecy didn't get him killed first.

Gabriel and Camael had started loading the car. Aaron was just about to shut the computer down when Mrs. Provost appeared in the doorway to the tiny office. "Don't shut that off right yet," she said. "I was thinking of maybe sending a note to my son."

Aaron got up and motioned for her to take the chair. "That would be nice. I'm sure he'd like to hear from you." He suddenly wondered if it could have been Leviathan that had kept her from leaving Blithe all these years.

"Damn thing'll probably blow up in my face," she said, scowling at the computer as she took a seat in front of the monitor.

"You'll do fine," he said. He then remembered that he hadn't paid the woman yet for his stay, and reached into his pocket for the money there. "Oh, before I forget," he said handing her the stack of bills. She took it from his hand and began to count it.

"Gave me too much," she said, handing back more than half the cash.

"You said that it was—"

"Are you calling me a liar, Corbet?" she interrupted with a scowl worse than the one she had given the computer.

Aaron knew he was on the edge of real trouble here. "No, it's just that you said—"

"Never mind what I said. This is plenty." She held up the money she had kept, then folded it and stuck it inside the front pocket of her ancient blue jeans. "I enjoyed your company—and your dog's, too, even though he's a bit of a pig, if you ask me."

Aaron laughed. "You don't have to tell me! The boy's been like that since he was a baby. His stomach's a bottomless pit."

They both laughed.

"Well, I gotta hit the road," Aaron said. "You take care of yourself, Mrs. Provost," he said, waving good-bye as he left the office doorway.

"Same to you, son," she said. "You and that dog of yours stop by again sometime, and bring your handsome friend along too."

Aaron headed for the front door, listening to

the old woman's fingers tentatively moving on the keyboard. It sounded as though she was doing just fine, but as he opened the door, he heard her curse and threaten the computer with being tossed out with the trash. Laughing softly to himself, he stepped from the house to join his friends.

Aaron was passing beneath the flowered archway to go to his car when he saw Katie McGovern. She was dressed in a baggy white T-shirt and some running shorts. The vet was patting Gabriel, checking out his bite wound. Aaron noticed that her hand was bandaged as well. "Hey," he said, approaching them and his dog.

"Hey, back," she answered. "Was out running and saw Gabriel in the yard. He begged me to come pet him. Healed up pretty fast, didn't he," she pointed out, running the flat of her bandaged hand along the dog's flank.

"I didn't tell her anything," Gabriel grumbled, looking at him guiltily, tongue lolling.

Aaron ignored the dog. "I don't think it was as bad as it looked—and plus, he had the best vet in town looking after him. How could he do anything but miraculously heal?" he asked, chuckling. They were both patting the Labrador now, and the animal was in his glory.

"So you're leaving, huh?" she said, eyeing his vehicle. He looked where she was staring and saw that Camael had already taken up his place in the front seat, patiently waiting.

"Yeah, got some things to take care of," he said, stroking Gabriel's side. "Thought I'd get an early start."

"Is that the friend you were waiting for?" she asked, motioning with her chin to the car, and the back of Camael's head.

"That's him. Got back from Portland yesterday," he lied.

"Nothing I could say to get you to stick around and help Kevin and me with the practice, is there?" she asked halfheartedly, already expecting that she knew what his answer would be.

"You and Kevin, eh?" he questioned, a sly smile creeping across his face.

"Yeah," she said, now rubbing Gabriel's ears. "Since he got back, we've been spending a lot of time with each other and have decided to give it another go." Katie shrugged. "We're taking it a day at a time—see what happens. So I guess your answer's no?"

Camael turned around in his seat and gave him an intense stare. *Even an angel's patience has its limits,* he thought, moving gradually toward the car. "Sorry," he said, opening the back door of the Toyota for Gabriel. "Still got something I have to do, but thanks for offering." He thought of his little brother still in the clutches of killer angels and he felt his pulse rate quicken. The dog jumped into the backseat, and he slammed the door closed.

"You're good, Aaron," she said, hands on her hips. "If you ever need a letter of recommendation for school or anything, be sure to look me up, okay?"

"Thanks," he said, opening the driver side door. "You take care now. I hope everything works out between you and Kevin."

Aaron sat behind the steering wheel and was just about to slam the door of the Toyota closed when Katie abruptly stopped him.

"The other night," she said, her eyes wide. She licked her lips nervously. "You know what happened then—don't you?" Katie nervously played with the bandage on her hand.

Aaron looked into her eyes and told her that he didn't know what she was talking about, but he suspected that she didn't believe him.

"There's a little voice in the back of my head telling me that I should be thanking you for something—but for the life of me I don't know why."

He turned the key in the ignition and started up the car. "You don't have to thank me," he said, shaking his head, feeling a little sad that he was leaving. The town of Blithe had really started to grow on him. His own little voice—the selfish one again—was telling him that he should turn the car off this instant, accept Katie's offer, and take up permanent residence in the now peaceful town—to turn his back on the prophecy.

"Never ignore the little voice in the back of your head, Aaron," she said, leaning into the open window and giving him a quick peck on the cheek. But he knew that it wasn't to be; that if he had listened, it would be no better than the false peace that he had known in the belly of Leviathan.

"Thank you," she said as she withdrew herself from the car.

"You're welcome," he responded, and she turned from the car with a final wave and continued with her morning run.

He had responsibilities now, he thought as he watched Katie recede down Berkely Street, duties that extended far beyond his own personal satisfaction and happiness. It was a lot to cope with, but what choice did he have, really? He'd tried to deny it, to keep it locked away, but that had almost got him killed. Begrudgingly, he was beginning to accept it was all part of what he had to do—the job he had been chosen for.

"I like her," Gabriel said as Aaron put the car in drive, beginning the process of turning the car around on the dead-end street. *"Even if she is a vet."*

"I like her too," Aaron said in the midst of completing a three-point turn, his mind already elsewhere. He thought about his brother, and the dangers that were obviously to come—and he thought about his father.

He began to drive up Berkely Street, and on reflex turned on the radio. Paul McCartney and the rest of the Beatles were singing "Yesterday." It had always been one of his favorite oldies, and listening to the words now, it had new meaning for him. He turned the volume up a bit and felt Camael's burning gaze upon him.

"I want you to listen to this," he said, glancing over at the scowling angel as he took a left off Berkely and headed back through the center of town. "Don't think of it as a song—think of it as poetry."

"I despise poetry," the angel growled, looking away from him to gaze out the passenger window at Blithe passing by.

"Bet you thought you hated French fries too," Aaron said, chuckling.

Would his life ever again be filled with lazy Sundays reading the newspaper, drinking milk, and eating doughnuts? Aaron had no idea what the future held, but he *did* know it would certainly be interesting; it was in the job description.

What else would one expect as a Messenger of God?

epilogue

$\mathcal{I}$t was a dream—but it felt like reality.

The night was cool, although she could feel the heat from the sand, warmed by the day's relentless sun, beneath her bare feet as she fled across the ocean of desert.

It seemed so real, as if part of a life lived in the past. Long, long in the past.

Her heart beat rapidly in her chest, and she turned back to gaze at the city burning in the distance—somehow she knew that its name was Urkish. The sky above the primitive desert-city had turned black, as smoke from the burning buildings of straw and mud rose to hide the stars.

She could hear a sound, a high-pitched, keening sound, and even at this distance, she had to cover her ears against it. It was like the cries of birds—hundreds of angry birds.

Each night the dreams became more vivid,

and she found she was beginning to fear sleep. She would have given anything for a dreamless night of rest. But it wasn't to be.

Someone called to her, and she remembered she wasn't alone. Eight others had fled Urkish with her—eight others had escaped from . . . from what? she wondered. A girl no older than she was, wrapped in a tattered cloak and hood, motioned frantically for her to follow. There was fear in her eyes, fear in all their eyes. What are they afraid of? What has driven us from the city? She wanted to know—she needed to know.

"Quickly," said the girl in a language the dreamer had never heard—yet could comprehend. "We must lose ourselves in the desert," the girl said as she turned back to the others, her ragged cloak blowing in the desert breeze. "It is our only chance." They started to run, fleeing across the dunes—but from what? the dreamer wondered again.

She turned her attention back toward the city. Was the answer there? The fires burned higher, and any semblance that a civilization had once thrived there was lost—consumed in the rising conflagration.

The others called to her, their voices smaller in the distance, carried on the wind. They pleaded for her to follow, but she did not move, her eyes fixed upon the city in flames.

Sadness enveloped her as she watched the city burn—as if Urkish was somehow important to her. Was it more than just a place she dreamed about? Did it actually have some kind of a special meaning for her?

She stamped her foot in the sand, frustration exploding within her. "I want to wake up," she shouted to the desert. "I want to wake up now." She closed her eyes, willing herself to the surface of consciousness, but the world of dream held her in its grasp.

The horrible cries again rang in her ears, and she opened her eyes. She saw them flying up from the fires of the city, their wings fanning the billowing black smoke as they rose. There were hundreds of them, and even from this distance she could see that they were clad in armor of gold.

She knew what they were. Ever since she was a child, they had filled her with wonder and contentment. She had fancied them her guardians, and believed they would never let any harm befall her.

Breathlessly she watched them fly now, dipping and weaving above the burning ruins of the city. She knew she'd been in this dream before, but for the life of her, could not remember why the heavenly beings had come to Urkish.

"They've come to kill you," said a whisper from the desert, and she knew the voice was right.

They were flying beyond the city now, out over the desert waste—searching. Searching for her.

She started to run, but the sand hindered her progress. Her heart hammered with exertion as she attempted to catch up with the others. She remembered now. She remembered how the creatures had dropped from the sky, fire in their hands—and the killing. She remembered the killing. Her thoughts raced with images of violence as she struggled to climb a dune, the sand giving way beneath her frantic attempts.

They were closer now—so very close. The air was filled with the sounds of pounding wings, and the cries of angry birds.

No, not birds at all.

She reached the crest of the dune. She could just about make out the others. She cried out to them, but the sound of her voice was drowned by the beating wings. She turned to look at them—to see how close they were.

And they were there, descending from the sky, descending from Heaven—screeching for her blood.

Angels.

How could she have ever loved creatures so heartless and cruel?

Vilma awoke from the nightmare, a scream upon her lips. She could still feel the wind on her face as they carried her up into the night sky, the swords of fire as they pierced her flesh.

She began to sob, burying her face in the pillow so her aunt and uncle would not hear her. They had already caught her crying twice this week and were beginning to worry. She couldn't blame them.

Getting a hold of her emotions, Vilma lifted her face from the pillow and caught something from the corner of her eye. Outside her bedroom window was a tree, and for the briefest moment there was something in that tree, something disturbingly familiar, and it had been watching her.

It was then that Vilma was convinced her aunt and uncle were right: She *did* have some kind of mental problem, and should probably seek help. Why else would she be having such horrible dreams—

And see angels outside her window.

His body covered in armor the color of blood, Malak the hunter crept through the beast's lair, searching for the scent of his prey. He removed the gauntlet of red from his hand and knelt before the ashen remains of the sea monster. Malak plunged his bare hand into the remnants of the beast, and just as quickly removed it. The hunter sniffed at the residue clinging to his fingers—his olfactory senses searching for a trace of the one his master sought. He hunted a special quarry, one that had meant something important to him long ago, in another life—before he was Malak.

There was a hint of the hunted upon his hand—but not quite enough.

He sensed that there were magicks in the air—spells to mask his enemy's comings and goings, but not enough to hide him from one as gifted as he was. His master Verchiel had blessed him with the ability to track any prey—and the myriad skills to vanquish them all. He was the hunter, and nothing would keep him from his quarry.

Malak stood and walked around the cave. He tilted his head back, letting the fetid air of the chamber fill his nostrils. His powerful sense of smell sorted the different scents, until he found the one he sought.

The hunter moved across the cavern, zeroing in on the source of the prized spore. He found it upon the wall of the cave, the tiniest trace of blood. He leaned into the wall, sniffing, but the blood had dried, which had taken away some of its pungent aroma. Malak leaned closer, his tongue snaking out from within the crimson facemask, to lick at the stain—his saliva reviving the blood's sharp, metallic stench.

The smell flooded his preternatural senses, and the hunter smiled. He now had the scent.

It was only a matter of time.

As many as one in three
Americans with HIV...
DO NOT KNOW IT.

More than half of those
who will get HIV this year...
ARE UNDER 25.

HIV is preventable.
You can help fight AIDS.
Get informed. Get the facts.

KNOW
HIV ▶ AIDS

www.knowhivaids.org
1-866-344-KNOW

FORCE
MAJEURE

TWENTY-YEAR-OLD GENIUS SHANE MONROE has his life laid out before him. As part of an accelerated program, he is working on a major research project to replicate a tornado through artificial means. When he manages to do just that, however, the course of his life is forever altered. His superiors want to know if he can do it "bigger—big enough to drop on an enemy village and call it an act of God."

Shane knows what he has to do. He shuts down his storm, switches majors, and leaves the lab behind.

He is midway through his next semester when he reads of a rash of natural disasters in South America. There is no doubt in his mind: This is his fault. His notes have been confiscated and his work replicated. Now Shane is on the run, from the government, friends, and even once-trusted mentors. What began as a reputable weather study has, with the force of a tornado, taken on an unstoppable life of its own . . . .

From best-selling authors
CHRISTOPHER GOLDEN
AND THOMAS E. SNIEGOSKI

Now Available from Simon Pulse

They're real,
and they're here...

When Jack Dwyer's best friend
Artie is murdered, he is devastated.
But his world is turned upside down
when Artie emerges from the ghostlands
to bring him a warning.

With his dead friend's guidance,
Jack learns of the Prowlers. They
move from city to city, preying on
humans until they are close to being
exposed, then they move on.

Jack wants revenge. But even as he
hunts the Prowlers, he marks himself—
and all of his loved ones—as prey.

Don't miss the exciting
new series from
BESTSELLING AUTHOR
CHRISTOPHER GOLDEN!

PROWLERS

AVAILABLE FROM SIMON PULSE
PUBLISHED BY SIMON ≡ SCHUSTER   3083-01